A PR

HARDS _ THE HEART

BOOK THREE

STEFANIE BRIDGES-MIKOTA

ABOUT THIS BOOK

When Glady Wimble's best laid plans crumble right in front of her eyes, can she fit the pieces of her dreams back together to transform herself into the person she wants to be?

Gladys Wimble is the spitting image of her mother and has the pretentiousness to prove it. Ashamed of who she's become and the people surrounding her who want to keep her in the same old box she wants to break out of, Gladys makes a huge and possibly reckless move.

She boards a train to Deer Lodge Montana - a rugged, makeshift mining community eons behind the town she came from. When she takes a teaching job, she thinks things might be looking up. But, once again, disaster looms on the horizon.

All Gladys wants is to become the person she's meant to be. But will anyone in this new ramshackle town give her that opportunity?

A NOTE FROM THE AUTHOR

Dear Readers,

The words in this book reflect the time period in which the story takes place. They do not reflect the personal views and beliefs of the author.

CHAPTER 1

Gladys Wimble was truly alone for the first time in her life. Everything was foreign, exciting, and terrifying at the same time.

When most her age were busy running households and growing the next generation, she chose a different path... Not one completely uncommon for a lady, but for a lady of her standing. The decision felt right when she first decided to make the move away from all she knew. Now that she was here, in a new town with new people, she wasn't so sure.

"And this is the gymnasium," Miss Dupont swiped her hand, palm up, in the large room.

Gladys looked her over as Miss Dupont was wrapping up the tour of the schoolhouse. She was a tall thin woman who looked to be in her upper twenties. Her nose was bent slightly as if it was broken at some point. Gladys couldn't quite decide if Miss Dupont's voice bordered on boredom or irritation.

"We hold lunch here when the weather turns too cold to be outside. Various community events also take place within these walls," she inserted as an afterthought.

Gladys turned her attention to the large room as she worked to absorb the vast information Miss. Dupont gave her.

"It's hard to imagine being too cold to be outside right now." Gladys smoothed her damp golden honey hair that had begun slipping out of its pins. Late summer heat combined with being stuck inside was miserable. She was ready to finish up for the day and cool down.

They had wandered through the rooms and Miss Dupont explained what each one was for and who would be in them before moving to the next. Gladys had been working in her room for a couple of days, but this was the first time she could see the whole building.

The school was large in the sense that it could hold around one hundred fifty students. There were only four main rooms with a couple small storage areas and an office. Gladys was told not to bother the storage rooms. They held equipment for the mine and, if needed, the miners would come for it.

The classrooms were sizable from what she was used to back home in Deer Lodge, Montana. A larger work environment wasn't the only thing she would need to get used to, either. Coming from a prosperous and notable family gave her a higher status from the start of her first teaching position. Here she was a nobody. She had to earn her way, and Gladys wasn't sure yet if she found that exciting or daunting.

Gladys was to teach the youngest group which consisted of kinders through second grade. Miss. Siller taught the next group and Miss Dupont was the oldest students' teacher.

"...the animals," Miss Dupont crossed her arms and tapped her toe, "Miss Wimble are you paying attention to me?" Miss Dupont snapped and glared down her crooked nose at her.

"Oh, sorry," Gladys turned her attention back to the woman. She found it hard to pay attention to her. Miss Dupont was harsh with her explanations and Gladys found her to be a no-nonsense cold person.

Unless she is only this way with me?

Gladys shook off that thought not wanting to cause troubles where there currently were none. "You said animals, but I apologize I didn't hear the first part."

"I will only go over this once, so please," she glared the last words to her, "do listen well."

"Yes, ma'am." Apparently, she was, and would be treated as, being the lowest on the totem pole. Gladys made a note to try and remember that Miss Dupont was the senior teacher here and clearly believed she should be treated as such. Gladys shivered despite the heat. This was the first time since moving that she felt an unease about her choice in being so far from home.

"The animals were in reference to the doors and the wild critters. Those doors must stay closed as some of the animals we share these woods with might try to find their way in."

Gladys was familiar with animals, but she never lived so close to "woods," as Miss Dupont called it. Deer Lodge did have forests around it, but there was more open farmland between town and forest. "Does that happen often? The animals approaching the school, I mean?"

Miss Dupont paused a moment assessing her, "No, and most of the animals are skittish of humans.

Bears have been known to get closer when food is scarce in the late winter and early spring. They smell ours and will try to get to it if they can. Some bears have learned to turn a doorknob with their mouths."

If Glady's doe-like eyes could have popped out of her head, they would have. "Bears? This close to town? And able to open doors?" Gladys really hoped that was Miss Dupont's attempt at humor.

"We do live in the middle of a forest. Have you looked around? The woods circle right at the edge of this town. Animals will wander through from time to time. We must do what we can to deter them, but confrontations do happen."

She did not want that to ever happen to her, so Gladys made a mental note to keep any and all doors shut at all times. "Thank you for the information. I will remember that."

"Good. See that you do. Now, I have my own room to finish preparing. Mr. Davis was here a little while ago as we were talking and left a sheet of paper on your desk that lists the rules you must follow. You will sign it and return it to me as I am to place it in your file. Just because we are in the middle of nowhere does not mean we do not hold ourselves to the standards of proper society." She turned on her heel and left Gladys behind, feeling dismissed and not sure how to take that last information.

If she judged Miss Dupont's temperament by history, Gladys would think she didn't like her. After all, she was being treated the way she used to treat others. Gladys sighed as she quietly reminded herself not to judge too quickly. She didn't know this person's past or if she was having a bad day today.

She took a deep breath and headed to her room to finish preparing for the first day of school and wondered as she walked how she didn't see Mr. Davis when Miss Dupont did. "Did I miss anything else?" Gladys spoke under her breath to herself. She hoped not, as she felt that Miss Dupont would not give many second chances.

She had already been busy working in her room before the tour and not much was left. She found the sheet Miss Dupont was referencing right where she said it would be. Scanning through, nothing out of the ordinary jumped out at her. The rules were similar here as anywhere. She couldn't be out after eight at night, she needed to wear dark modest dresses, riding in a buggy with a single man was forbidden, she couldn't marry and keep her job, no visiting certain establishments, and listed were the cleaning duties for the day and week. She signed it and left it on her desk to return to Miss Dupont when she finished for the day.

Gladys set to work finishing her tasks and before too long she decided to call it a day. Between the work in here, focusing on Miss Dupont, and trying to put to memory everything she had been told, she was tired, too hot, and ready to be done.

Gladys set the broom in the corner close to the door. She took one last look over her classroom and decided she was satisfied. She had dusted and swept, readied the fireplace, cleaned the chalkboard, and made sure she had her water pail with tin cup, as well as other necessary items in place.

The desks had been arranged and rearranged until she approved of the final configuration. Grabbing her bag and the paper, she closed the door, realizing the next time she opened it would be to greet her new class. With signed paper in hand, she made her way to Miss Dupont, then was on her way along the dusty dirt road back to Mr. and Mrs. Davis' home.

Since she'd arrived, Gladys had been staying with Mr. Davis and his wife. The two other teachers lived together in a small home close by, but Gladys was to be housed in various homes until a more permanent solution could be found.

On that first night, Mr. Davis informed her that she would rotate through different homes changing every month. This setup made her a bit nervous as she had never lived with anyone other than her parents. Gladys worked to push down those nerves, and it did take some effort. She knew if she was ever going to run her own life and be independent, she would need to keep her chin up and push through.

Mr. Davis' home was nothing fancy, but it was comfortable. He was a pumpman in the mine. Gladys knew that meant he pumped water, but she was still learning how the mining operation worked and thus didn't fully understand the whole of his job. So far, the only things she knew were that they were mining for coal, and they ran on the whistles that blared twice a day every day.

Mrs. Davis, a sweet middle-aged woman, was preparing the evening meal. Gladys found her apron, rolled up her sleeves, and took over rolling out dough for biscuits. "It sure smells good in here."

"Yes, it does, I'm hungry." Mrs. Davis placed her hand on her stomach as it growled, and both ladies laughed. "Did you have a pleasant day today?"

Gladys used a mug to form the biscuits and continued speaking. "I did. I believe the room is as ready as it could ever be."

Mrs. Davis was pulling the venison roast out of the oven. "That's great, given that school is just a few days away. Tell me, are you nervous at all?"

"Oh, I'm always nervous to start a new year. I think this year more so though, given I am not familiar with any of the students."

"Well, that will change soon enough." Mrs. Davis stopped with a smile on her face. "We are having company tonight."

Gladys's excitement grew a little with that news. "Who do I get to meet tonight?"

"Why, just the people you will be living with starting tomorrow."

Gladys swallowed a lump that had formed in the back of her throat. "Tomorrow? I thought I would have a couple more days here first."

"Well, with school starting Monday morning, Mr. Davis felt it was important for you to settle in a bit and meet some of your students."

"My students? This family has more than one in my class?"

Mrs. Davis stirred mashed potatoes that were keeping warm on the stove to prevent them from scorching. "Yes, Sadie is the youngest and will be in your younger group. Jeffrey is a little older. I can't remember their ages exactly, but you will find out tonight when you meet them."

Gladys's hunger vanished and instead was replaced with butterflies. She hoped this was a nice family. Especially since she would be lodging with them.

Mrs. Davis put her arm around Gladys shoulders. "Relax dear. All will be well, you will see."

Gladys tried, but failed. She spent the next hour mentally trying to prepare for this very important dinner. Before she knew it, a knock sounded on the door.

"Oh dear, it seems they are here already, and they beat Charles home." She undid her apron and headed to the front door. Gladys stayed behind to finish the meal prep and calm her breathing.

Four people crowded into the front room and Gladys could hear children's voices. About that time, she heard Mrs. Davis call for her.

Gladys untied her apron, folded it, and placed it on the counter before following the sounds. She paused in the door and Mrs. Davis approached her to make the introductions. The children stood quietly waiting.

"Everyone, this is Miss Wimble. Miss Wimble this is Mr. and Mrs. Crowley and their children

Jeffrey and Sadie." Jeffrey nodded his head when his name was called, and Sadie did a little curtsy bob at her name.

Gladys gave the children a smile. Jeffrey stood about a foot taller than little Sadie. His hands were tucked into his pockets and his expression was one of disinterest. His chestnut hair was ruffled and there were freckles splashed across his nose. Sadie was quite the opposite. Her dark hair was plaited down the back and her smile glowed on her pale flawless skin. "It's a pleasure to meet you all."

Mrs. Crowley spoke first of the group. "The pleasure is ours. Sadie here has been very excited to finally meet you. This will be her first year in school. Jeffrey will be in the second grade."

Gladys bent down to be closer to the height of her students. "I'm very glad to meet you, Sadie and Jeffrey. I hope we have a great school year together."

"Awe, shucks, do I have to go to school?" Jeffrey looked over at his pa.

"Yes, son, you do, and you will not talk that way in front of your teacher." Mr. Crowley gave his son a stone-faced stare and Jeffery quickly changed his attitude.

"I'm real excited, miss. I love school. I want to learn everything." Sadie was beginning to ramble.

"Oh Sadie, you say that now. You've never been to school before. How can you know you love it?" Jeffrey quickly looked at his father and clamped his mouth shut again.

Gladys couldn't help but chuckle, although she attempted to contain it. "I'm sure we are going to have a splendid time together. Sadie, did you know that the two of you are the first student's I've met?"

"We are?" The little girl's eyes grew to the size of saucers and a giant smile formed on her small face.

"Yes, you are. I can tell we are going to get along nicely ."

Gladys took her hand and the group made their way to the table just as Charles arrived. He apologized for being late, something about the mine. Gladys wasn't listening because she was in deep conversation with her new favorite pupil.

CHAPTER 2

Gladys woke the next morning excited for the next month's arrangement. She worked quickly to help Mrs. Davis prepare and clean up breakfast. She packed her mother's quilt from the bed she was using, her brush, and perfume she'd made from the flowers that grew in her mother's garden into her trunk. She chose not to bring many items with her in the beginning as she wasn't sure what she would need and what she wouldn't. She could always send for them later.

Now, knowing she was boarding with families, she was thankful she chose to do that. The homes were small, and each family would have everything she would need. Gladys could send for her things once she had a more permanent residence.

"I'm ready when you are Gladys," Mr. Davis hollered from the front room.

Gladys walked out and let him know she was packed up and ready to go. Mr. Davis flung her trunk on his shoulder and led her outside. The day was bright and sunny. There was too much bare dirt for Gladys' taste, but she had an idea to help change that. She had something tucked away in her trunk that was just the ticket to combat that little problem. And she had close to forty little helping children to make the task go quickly. Timing was the only issue at hand preventing the project from starting.

They made their way down the row of identical wooden homes before stopping at one and knocking on the door. Gladys paused to count so she would remember which one to come to. There was nothing she could see that would identify any of them.

Sadie opened the door with her mother close on her heels. The little angel bounded over the threshold and wrapped Gladys in a hug so tight it caught her off guard, forcing her to take a step back to balance herself.

"Oh, you're here, you're here, you're here!" the little girl exclaimed.

Gladys joyfully laughed. "Yes, I'm here." She wrapped her arms around Sadie and squeezed her.

Sadie pushed back and grabbed her hand pulling her in and past her mother.

"Sadie, please!" Mrs. Crowley reprimanded her daughter.

"Sorry, Momma." She dropped her hand and let Gladys compose herself a moment.

"I'm so sorry, Miss Wimble, she is clearly very excited about you living with us." Mrs. Crowley scowled at Sadie, which made the little girl lower her head.

"Sorry, Miss Wimble."

Gladys' heart melted for a moment when Sadie's apologetic eyes met hers.

"It's really all right, Mrs. Crowley. Please, call me Gladys." She smiled at Sadie who raised her head and beamed back at her.

"Hi, Gladys!" Sadie tested her name out.

Both ladies laughed. Gladys bent down in front of Sadie, "Well Sadie, I'll tell you what. When we are here at your home you may call me Gladys, but at school I must be Miss Wimble. Understand?"

Sadie shook her head, "Yes, miss."

Mr. Davis cleared his throat. He remained

standing on the stoop with Gladys' trunk slung over his shoulder.

"Oh dear, please come in. I'll show you where to place that." Mrs. Crowley led them in and had Mr. Davis follow her behind a door. They both stepped back out into the main area.

"Thank you for volunteering to house our new teacher Mrs. Crowley. I sure do appreciate that."

She followed him to the door. "The pleasure is ours. We are happy to help out."

Mr. Davis looked back at Gladys. "If you need anything you know where to find me. The other two teachers should be able to help as well."

"Thank you for the hospitality these last few days and for the opportunity to teach here. I am very excited to get started." Gladys looked down at Sadie who remained quiet while the adults spoke.

Mr. Davis headed home and left the women to get better acquainted. Mrs. Crowley asked if Gladys would like a cup of tea and Gladys gladly accepted. Sadie tugged on Gladys's hand and motioned for her to come closer. Gladys bent down, and Sadie cupped her hand over her mouth while standing on tiptoe to reach Gladys' ear.

"You are sleeping with me!" She tried to say it in

a whisper, but she was so excited she struggled to control the volume.

Mrs. Crowley overheard. "Sadie, please go outside and play for a while."

"Yes, Momma," she smiled one last time at Gladys and ran for the door.

Mrs. Crowley brought a steaming mug of black tea, "Most in these parts prefer coffee, but I am partial to tea. We have some honey, if you would like to sweeten it?"

Gladys took the mug. "I would love some honey Mrs. Crowley."

"Oh, please, call me Sylvia, dear. We will be getting to know each other very well over the next month. No sense in formalities." She retrieved the honey and placed it on the table before gesturing for Gladys to take a seat. They both settled in and took a sip of their very hot tea.

"What Sadie told you is correct. You will be bunking with her. I do hope that is okay. This house has two rooms. James, that is Mr. Crowley, and I are in one and the children share the other. They each have their own beds of course. When they get older I will need to use a sheet to divide the space."

Gladys had never slept with anyone before. She wasn't sure if she was comfortable with that or not.

She was very happy, though, knowing she had a bed to sleep in. The floor was not an appealing option and she hoped she never had to deal with that.

"I'm sure it will be just fine." She tried to sound confident if not for her sake, but for Sylvia's as well. This family was being very generous and Gladys would work to remember that.

In her past, she was quick to judge and look down on those not equal to her in social ranking. This family would have been put in the poor group, also known as a group she wouldn't have associated with. Her mother would have never allowed her to be more than acquaintances or superficial friends.

"I want to thank you for allowing me to stay here. I would like to be as helpful as possible. Anything you would like me to do, just ask."

Sylvia placed her mug on the table. "There really isn't more work than I can handle here, but I would appreciate the company and the help. I have a garden out back that I tend every couple days. Cooking and cleaning as well as mending occur daily. I do make extra bread every week and give it to the bachelors. One lives right next door here." She paused and thought a moment. "Actually, he probably could use more help than I need."

She didn't elaborate, and Gladys didn't push

further. "My mother has a magnificent garden and I'm very adept and used to spending time managing that. Unfortunately, I don't have much skill where mending is concerned, although I have made many quilts. My parents paid to have my clothing fixed or just bought new." She cringed, hoping that didn't come out sounding conceited.

"That's just fine. It's just mainly repairing the knees in Jeffrey's pants. That boy is constantly putting holes in them. I can teach you if you are interested."

Gladys thought for a moment and agreed that it was a skill she should have already known and thanked her for offering.

"I'm sure you will need regular time to plan your lessons and such. You can work in my room after supper is cleaned up so the children won't be a bother."

Gladys took that to mean she would be required to help with cleanup and most likely prep too. That was fine with her. She wasn't a strong cook, which made it another area for her to learn some. "Yes, thank you."

The ladies finished their tea and Sylvia led Gladys into her new room. It was small with two beds on opposite walls and a small walkway between them. It felt cozy. Jeffrey's bed was closest to the door and had a crazy quilt on it. Sadie's was topped with a delicate looking quilt of pale lavenders and greens trimmed with a ruffle. The bed was narrow, and Gladys hoped the two of them could fit nicely in it.

Gladys' trunk had been placed along the wall opposite Sadie's bed. She would leave her own quilt tucked inside. Based on the eagerness she had already shown her, Sadie probably wouldn't mind if Gladys used her own quilt, but she felt she was imposing enough on these children. She also thought once she started assigning homework and expecting things from them, Sadie may change her mind on how much she liked her.

"This is a beautiful room. I especially love Sadie's quilt."

Sylvia smiled. "My mother made that for her. She passed a little over a year ago."

"Oh, I'm sorry to hear that." Gladys felt a bit awkward not knowing exactly what to say.

Pausing a moment, Sylvia tucked a loose auburn lock behind her ear and folded her arms across her stomach. "It's okay. She was up in years and went peacefully in her sleep." She sighed. "I'll give you some privacy and let you settle in for a bit. I'll go clean up our tea."

Sylvia left Gladys alone. She wasn't sure what she was supposed to do to settle in. She didn't have much and being here only a month plus sharing a room meant she couldn't take over any space. She did have her trunk though and decided she could use that as a table top. She removed her perfume and other personal items and placed them on top of the trunk making sure to leave room for her dress to rest there when she was sleeping. Her Sunday best was in her trunk, as well as a couple of other work dresses and some undergarments. She looked around again and tested out the bed, which proved to be comfortable, before returning to see what she could help with.

The rest of the day was spent touring the small, but beautiful garden, helping prepare food, and taking a walk to continue familiarizing herself with the town. All different languages surrounded her. Most of the people were immigrants, but the ones she met, so far, knew English well enough to communicate with her.

Many kids were out playing, and she did meet most of them with help from Sadie. They seemed like wonderful children. She hoped that first impressions proved true.

By the evening, her first day at her new home was better than she had expected. This first month was going to go nicely, as long as she could sleep well with sharing the bed. It would only be a matter of an hour or two before she learned how that would go. She decided not to fret about the future, however near it may be, and settled in to listen to Mr. Crowley sit by the fire and tell his children a bedtime story.

CHAPTER 3

*G*ladys awoke Monday morning to a beautiful blue sky and chirping birds. Normally, she would start on breakfast while Sylvia made the fire and got the children moving, but not today.

Sylvia knew she would be nervous and have more to do this morning than others, so she gave her the morning off from helping. Gladys was grateful. It meant she had more time in the classroom before the children arrived. The first day of school had given her butterflies before but being at a new school felt like it was her first year all over again.

Over the past couple of days, Gladys had learned that the school in Ravensdale, Washington started off like most. In its beginning, it was a one-room schoolhouse that had to quickly convert into a three-room school, complete with gymnasium.

The logging, and most recently, mining businesses, made the town swell to bulging before they rebuilt. Most of the town was owned by the mining company itself. Georgetown, adjacent to Ravensdale, was a place Gladys was not allowed. It held the businesses of ill repute where the single miners and some married miners chose to spend their precious extra coins.

Between Miss Dupont and Mr. Davis, the school's director, she was overwhelmed with information about the town's history and the current school set up.

⸙

UPON ARRIVING AT THE SCHOOL, she immediately filled the drinking bucket with water before moving to the blank chalkboard to write her name. When the weather turned chilly, she would need to start the fire, but the days were still warm enough that it was not yet necessary.

Gladys was told all the children would bring their own slate. There were not enough readers for each to have their own, so those would be shared.

Having kindergarten through second grade would mean many students would not be as independent as the older kids. She would need to pair up those who learned quickly with those who didn't. She would give the younger kids an older partner. The younger group would like that but wasn't sure how the older ones would feel about it.

Gladys was writing the week's spelling words for each grade on the board when the first sounds of little voices began making their way to the room.

She put her chalk down and made sure that her smile reached her eyes. Even though she was nervous, the children didn't need to know. They would be nervous themselves without her adding to it. The students began filing in, most were silent watching her. Gladys was sure they were curious about her and unable to hide their inquisitive gazes. She could see some lean close and whisper to each other. Hopefully it was all pleasant.

"Good morning. Won't you please come in. Kindergarten will sit up front, first grade in the middle, and second graders in the back please." She watched the children take their seats as a few more were entering from the back. Sadie came up to her and stood by her, "Sadie dear, you need to go take a seat in the front there." Gladys pointed to the appropriate spot.

"I was hoping to help you, Gladys." Sadie clasped her hands in front of her and was making the skirt of her dress swish side to side.

Gladys bent down and gave a gentle tug on one of her raven braids. "Remember, I'm Miss Wimble here. I know you want to help dear, but while we are here you are a student like everyone else.

Sadie hung her head a bit, "I'm sorry, Gla- Miss Wimble. I will try to remember." She raised her head up with hopeful eyes, "Can I help you after school?"

"Only if your momma didn't say to come straight home. I don't mind if you stay with me and go home when I do, but only if your parents approve of that first." Gladys stood back up, "Okay now, you go take your seat."

Sadie did as she was told, and Gladys paused looking at the children before introducing herself. She made the error of asking if anyone had any questions for her.

Multiple hands shot up in the air and she realized she would need to limit how many she took, or she would be answering questions for much longer than the time she allotted. Questions ranged from about her specifically to about the class.

They wanted to know where she came from, if she was married, which then had many children laughing and blurting out that's why she was a Miss and not a Mrs., how old she was, how much homework they would have, if they were going to play games. The children took the opportunity to ask questions seriously and made sure they didn't miss out. There were also the inevitable stories rather than questions. Those she had to cut short.

Once Gladys finally regained control of her class- room, she moved onto the next order of business, rules. They started with the older kids offering what the past teacher's rules were. Gladys made note of which ones she was keeping and which she would toss. Then she added the rest of hers to it.

The rules included: no running, raising hands to talk, being helpful, not laughing at someone's questions, (which she decided to implement after the scene from earlier), arriving promptly and ready for learning each day, and doing anything and everything asked with pride.

She went into detail about what those meant and explained what the consequences were for misbehaving. Then she told the kids to think of two things they would like for her to know about them. They would each take turns saying their name and their two interesting details about themselves.

Gladys had a journal and opened to a sheet where she had already drawn out the seating chart. She added the names as the children spoke. After the whole class finished, she told them they would be staying in these seats until she had all their names down. Having almost forty students would take a while to remember their names. She had two, Sadie and Jeffrey, down already and that was a good start.

Once the business portions were finished for the day they could start on lessons. It would take a while for Gladys to learn where everyone currently was in their education.

The first several days would be spent asking questions and having each child respond, verbally or on their slates, so she could determine how to group them accordingly. It was a tedious process but it must be done in order to fully understand the starting point of each child and how to help each student progress.

Lunch came faster than Gladys thought. The morning seemed to race by. She was hungry, though, and dismissed the children to sit outside and eat before playing. They needed to run off some energy.

Gladys sat at her desk to eat her lunch in some

much needed quiet. Her class was full, but so far things seemed to go smoothly. For that she was grateful and that her nerves had calmed considerably. They had an hour for lunch, so Gladys finished hers, set up the afternoon portion of school, and then walked outside to see how the children were getting along.

The whole school was outside, which made for some chaos, but the other two teachers were there as well. Gladys was able to catch up on their morning and it seemed the whole school was running well. All three teachers made their way back to their rooms ahead of the students. One of the oldest girls had a pocket watch and was instructed to ring the bell at the appropriate time.

The second half of the day seemed to be moving right along until a barking sound was heard in the distance. She tried to teach over it, but the bark was growing louder and many of the kids were looking around trying to figure out where it was coming from. Before she knew it, the dog rushed into the classroom. The children squealed with delight and the dog was very excited, making its rounds to all the kids. Just after a tall lanky man appeared at her door.

"Sorry to disturb, ma'am. Lady, get over here!" He

shouted using an accent Gladys had not heard before. He began chasing the dog around the room and the dog was trying very hard to not be caught.

"I presume this is your dog, sir?" Gladys was yelling above all the noise.

"It is, yes," he replied sounding a bit out of breath. "It seems someone left the door open and she took off and now here she is. I'm very sorry."

"Well," looking around she realized she needed to get order to her class, so the dog would calm down and this strange man could catch her. Gladys banged on her desk much like a judge would do, but she used a heavy dictionary instead of a gavel. The children looked her way when she spoke. "Children, please sit and be quiet. I know you are excited, but dogs are not allowed in school. Let this man get his dog so he can be on his way and we can resume lessons."

Most of the children obeyed. A few struggled to calm down and she approached them and assisted. The dog had stopped running between desks and the man was able to subdue the dog and fitted his belt around the dog's neck for a collar. The children couldn't help but snicker at the sight of the skinny man with a dog in one hand and the back of his britches in the other as he made his way to the door.

After another apology they were off, and Gladys was able to get back to teaching.

Fortunately, the rest of the day brought no more intrusions. They were able to finish all Gladys had planned, but with more effort than it should have required. The children would giggle at random times which set off a chain reaction through the room. As much as she, too, could picture the spectacle of the unexpected visitor, she did her best to rein in the bunch.

Gladys dismissed them to go home before she began her after-school tasks. She was tired and ready for a good meal and to rest her feet. With chores yet to do, that time would be a while yet coming. She sighed and got back to work. She hadn't worked very long when a knock sounded at the door.

"Oh, what now?" She put down her chalk and opened the door in the back of the room to find the same lanky man from before, this time without his dog and with his belt back in its place.

"My children have left for the day. You'll have to come back tomorrow if you wish to disrupt again." Gladys was trying to focus on the interruption less the humorous aspect of it all.

His eyebrows shot up and for a moment forgot

why he came, "I just wanted to come back and say a proper apology without my dog with me."

"Well, mister, you wouldn't know how long it took to get the kids completely under control, and for the rest of the day I kept having to bring them to attention." Her hands were on her hips and she was tapping her foot.

"Yes, well, I am real sorry, ma'am. I just wanted to be sure to do the Christian thing, which is to right my dog's wrong," he was a bit irritated at her attitude and turned to leave before she could comment.

Gladys slumped in the closest seat to the door. She had messed that up by reverting to her old ways and he made sure to point out her error.

Would this day ever end?

She took a deep breath and stood while brushing out her skirt. The classroom was clean enough. She needed to head home and forget this afternoon ever happened. Tomorrow was a new day. She hoped upsetting that man wouldn't interrupt her ability to earn the friendship from others within the community .

CHAPTER 4

The next several days at school went without a hitch. Gladys was thankful for that. The dog hadn't been seen again. During lunch the day after the incident, she sat with the other two teachers and explained what had happened. Miss Dupont had the oldest group of students and confirmed that she would speak to her class about checking the door every day when entering after lunch. Gladys still felt awful for the way she handled the situation. She was rude to that man and knew she needed to apologize but wasn't aware of how to make that happen. She never got his name.

The two teachers besides herself, Miss Dupont and Miss Siller, had taught together for a few years. Gladys was able to find that much out, but they didn't reveal much else. Miss Siller was shorter, but not overly so. She was more round, with wide hips. The most notable feature of her, though, was her hair. It was kinky curly. Both women were quiet, kept to themselves it seemed. Gladys hoped she could find a way to make friends with them, but so far, her attempts gotten her nowhere.

Gladys had been bunking with Sadie for a couple weeks and her sore body was proof. She wasn't sleeping well. She hoped the next house had a bed just for her, but she knew better than to wish for the next to impossible. Unless she was with a childless family or one of the executives that lived in the larger homes, she feared it would be much of the same. Sadie proved to be a quick learner. Working with her at home helped. Maybe instead of wishing to be in a place that gave her a bed to herself, she should be hoping to be placed with students who could use extra help.

Teaching was Gladys' passion. She had secretly wished to become a teacher early on, but due to her mother's ideas, never shared it. She kept that part of her tucked away in the safety of her own heart. It took years for her to gain the courage, but once she did, there was no going back.

Her mother never outright stopped her, her

father wouldn't let her, but she did question every-thing Gladys had done, and tried to chip away at her happiness piece by piece. She couldn't be touched at school, though. The joy she felt each day erased all her mother's words.

Moving away and not dealing with that during evening and breaks made her heart sing even more. This was something of her own, something she set out to do without the influence from anyone else. She was proud of her work, and every little achieve-ment a child made increased her pride, encouraged her to continue, and nourished her love of it.

Gladys woke Sunday to go to church. Her current boarding family was Catholic, so she attended with them. She had yet to establish herself in a church and thought mingling with them all before settling on one, would be wise. Seeing which children went where would give her more insight into their personal lives as well.

St. Barbara's was small, but lovely and newly built. The church was in the neighboring town of Black Diamond. Ravensdale had an even newer Catholic church built the previous year, but the Crowley's loved the community that had formed in this one and hadn't yet wanted to change.

The church had a tall steeple that housed a large

brass bell that was clanging for the community. Inside held rows of pews for the parishioners to sit on. Gladys followed behind the children and joined in their pew several rows back from the front. This was her second time attending. The service was performed in Latin, but she had a pamphlet that had both Latin and English written, so she could follow along.

After service, many attendees stayed and had fellowship together. The children ran around getting some energy out after being still and patient during services. They stayed for a short time before heading for home. Gladys headed out to the garden and sat amongst the vegetables and few flowers.

Sylvia came out and joined Gladys where she sat. "I hoped I would get a chance to speak with you without the children."

"Oh, what's on your mind?" Gladys was picking some clovers out of the ground from between the flowers.

"Well, we've both been busy, and I was just wondering how your first couple of weeks have gone."

Gladys thought for a moment before answering, "The children are lovely. I'm really enjoying my time with them."

"And what about everything else?" Sylvia prompted, hoping Gladys would reveal a bit more about herself.

Gladys thought she should know already without having to tell her. Besides school, she was here. She didn't have a life, yet.

"So far I haven't made any friends. I was hoping to hit it off with at least one of the two teachers, but they seem to keep to themselves."

Sylvia sighed. "I see. I'm sure it will come in time. You are new. People will take a while to feel you out before they open themselves up to you."

She thought about that for a bit. "Hopefully that's all it is. I just get this odd feeling that there is something they aren't telling me. Little looks between themselves."

Sylvia patted Gladys' knee, "I'm sure it's nothing. Those two have been here a few years now and are respected in their positions within the community, although not very friendly in general with anyone. It was too bad they couldn't fit you in with them. They do have tight quarters, though. Hopefully, a solution gets figured out sooner than later. I would like to see you settled in more, maybe even feel at home. Sadie would sure love for you to be a permanent neighbor here."

Gladys smiled at her, "Thanks. I hope I do, too. I would dearly love to find permanent housing soon. Sadie is a sweet thing during the day, but at night she becomes a flailing animal." She closed her lips wishing she hadn't said that out loud then tried to laugh it off. She was very thankful for them putting her up and didn't want to sound ungrateful.

Sylvia chuckled. "I'm sorry about that. She has always been that way. Maybe I could move her to the floor."

"Oh no, please," Gladys interrupted. "I don't want to push her out of her bed. I've survived half my time here, I'm sure I'll get through the rest just fine.

Both ladies chuckled.

Sylvia's eyebrows pinched together in thought. "Gladys, I was wondering how you might feel about taking on another job to increase your funds and get you into your own place sooner."

"Really? I'm not sure how much time I have, but what did you have in mind?" She was intrigued by the prospect.

Sylvia was now also picking at the weeds between them. "Well, I know a single man close to us that could probably use a house cleaner once a week. Now, it wouldn't be proper for you to be there with him alone. But he works shifts and when he was on and you had free time of course, maybe you could spend some time tidying up for him?"

Gladys was silently absorbing this and tossing the idea around. "That is an idea. If I can squeeze it in and he is open to it, I will consider it further."

"Oh good," she sighed, "Seeing as how I already asked him." She shrugged her shoulders as though asking for forgiveness or bracing for Gladys' reaction.

Gladys was taken aback. She was used to her mother asserting herself in her life. Having someone else do it felt as if a privacy line had been crossed. She silently chastised herself though. Sylvia was just being thoughtful. She meant no harm. "I guess that means he said he would like that?"

Sylvia nodded in great apprehension.

Gladys looked to the heavens. "All right. If we can find a time that meets both of our schedules, I'll do it."

An audible release of breath gushed from Sylvia. "Oh good. He was quite excited at the prospect. Most of the women here are married and tending their own families. The single men must fend for them- selves in some areas. I do try to take over some extra food here and there. The boarding house provides meals but having something extra is nice.

They all work so hard and I feel bad they must come home to do all that work as well."

Gladys didn't mention that she worked all day and came home to have a list of to dos herself as well. Her work wasn't as physical of course, but she still had days that she was exhausted. Loving the work helped to keep her going though. "You know my schedule. Talk it over and let me know what will work for him. I'll start as soon as we agree."

Sylvia got to her feet and after thanking Gladys for being open to this, left her alone in the garden. It was after she left, Gladys realized she didn't ask how much she would be working or what would be expected. She could assume though. She supposed she would figure it out all in due time. She did hope it would work out. Having her own place would mean her own workload would increase. She would be tending to all her own meals, her own laundry, her own house duties, as well as her teaching duties. Having her own bed would be worth it though.

CHAPTER 5

The next few weeks passed without any fuss. Gladys had formed a nice routine at school and in the Crowley's home. Soon she would be moving on to her next home and that thought saddened her. She had formed a bond with Sadie and only seeing her at school was a sad thought to consider.

Gladys was excited at the prospect of getting more sleep, though, as Sadie was still tossing and turning. Many nights Gladys was awakened with a knee to the back or an arm flopped onto her trunk. She had a few bruises to prove it, too. She would not let on to Sylvia again about the issue. She still felt horrible for bringing it up in the first place.

No more dogs made any appearances in school,

for which she was grateful, but that also meant she didn't know who the gentleman was and couldn't right her wrong.

Another issue that was becoming more evident was the lack of relationship between her and the other teachers. Gladys had tried to reach out during lunch and after school, but they seemed to be busy doing other things or absent when she went searching. Her earlier feelings of there being an issue had grown, but she hoped maybe they were just very busy. The beginning of school was always an active time and the large classes only added to the full and hectic schedule.

Gladys had dismissed class for the day and was sitting at her desk trying to find new ways to teach the students who were just beginning to learn English. Since the majority of the families here were immigrants, several of the students did not speak or understand English at an appropriate level for their age. Having such a mixed class added to the problem. She needed to spend time working with them, but that meant taking away time to further the progress of those at a higher level. She had hoped to speak with the other teachers to get ideas, but that hadn't been possible yet. She was just thinking of approaching Mr. Davis about the issue when he walked through the door.

"Good afternoon, Miss Wimble."

Gladys stood "Hello! I was just thinking about seeing you to ask for your advice."

"Well, what can I help you with?" He replied as he walked to the front row and sat a bit awkwardly in the too small desk.

She walked over to the desk next to him and sat a bit more comfortably than he did. "I have several students who are not at grade level in English. I'm not exactly sure how to help them improve without slowing down those who are progressing."

Mr. Davis paused for a moment, mulling over the issue. "Well, as you know, I'm not a teacher. I've never been trained. I just run the school. Have you asked the other teachers? Maybe they will have some insight."

She sighed. "I have tried, but I keep missing them. Or when they are here, there is not time to converse."

"I see. What about when you go on your trip this weekend?"

Gladys was confused, "Trip? What trip?"

Mr. Davis paused, "You don't know? I thought all three of you were going."

"All three? Three who?" Then it dawned on her who he was speaking about. "Oh, the three teachers?"

He stood and walked over to the window to look out. A look of puzzlement crossed his face. "Yes, I was asked if the teachers could have a day to go to the market, which I agreed with. School has started smoothly and a day off and out of town, I thought, would be nice. I assumed it was for all of you. I guess it's just the other two, though."

"Oh!" Gladys slouched in a defeated way.

He turned and faced her, "I'm sorry. I'm not sure why you didn't know. Maybe they just haven't had the time yet to ask you."

"Yes, maybe." She knew better. She used to be the girl who was on the other end. She hadn't felt what being excluded was like and she decided it was a horrible feeling. Gladys had tried to reach out to them. She wasn't sure what more she could do. Maybe, in time, it would be easier. She could hope anyway .

"I'm really sorry I can't help with your issue. If I see one of the other two teachers, I will let them know you would love some ideas." He tipped his head for a good day and turned to leave before turning back. "Oh, I almost forgot." he reached into his pocket and pulled out an envelope. "This came in the mail for you."

Gladys took the envelope and Mr. Davis excused himself. She looked at the front noticing it was from her mother. After what she just found out she really didn't want to deal with what may or may not be written in the letter.

Feeling the other teachers' rejection made her realize she had yet to make a real friend. Mrs. Davis and Sylvia were wonderful, but she wasn't close with them either. They were friendly, but she didn't feel like she could share this with them. A feeling of complete aloneness washed over her.

Maybe it was payback. Maybe she deserved this or she had earned it. Whatever the case, she hoped it wasn't a lifetime of punishment. She didn't like the friends she had back home, as they were superficial friends, but for right now they were better than none.

She stood, wiped her eyes, and took a deep cleansing breath. She couldn't think about school anymore, so she decided to take a walk, tucking the envelope away to open when she was feeling a bit better.

The weather was still warm in the day, but with October just around the corner she knew that wouldn't last too much longer. Many of the children were playing outside and, as she passed, they would run up and greet her.

She observed them at play. They were friends to each other. She could see them engaging with one another -- being friendly and helpful seemed natural to them. Meanness and rudeness that Gladys used to partake in was a learned behavior. She could remember a time early on when she wanted to play with everyone. Her mother directed her with who was acceptable and who would never be invited. It was a subtle teaching. The rules were never blatantly laid out for her. She was crafty about it.

Gladys continued her walk. She noted that the town had gone up in a rush. Stumps from felled trees dotted the landscape. The train ran right in between the businesses and the homes. It was loud, and Gladys still wasn't used to living that close to the tracks. She hoped her next home was farther away but had yet to learn whom she would be living with.

Ravensdale had around one thousand people. The town had everything one needed. She would love to have seen Tacoma. Maybe one day she would make herself go. The train ride wasn't long at all but going by herself felt scary. Gladys chuckled to herself thinking about that as she made her way all the way from Montana to here and wasn't scared. She was excited. Now she struggled to find that excitement about being here.

Turning a corner, she decided to head for her current home. The garden was calling her. She needed a distraction to stop her negative thoughts. Working in her mother's garden always calmed her.

It was the only time her mother allowed her to get a bit dirty. Gardening was acceptable work for a female in her mother's eyes, so long as it wasn't gardening out of necessity, but for passion or pastime. Getting her hands dirty, she hoped, would be just the thing to cheer her up.

The flowers helped, like usual. Gladys took out the envelope from her mother and decided to read it.

MY DEAREST GLADYS,

Oh, I do miss you. Life isn't the same here without you. Your father is driving me mad, like usual, really. I don't understand why you insist upon working and why you needed to move so far away to do it. Really, dear, you could be doing so much in your community right here, if you were married well, of course. The women's league is looking for more teachers. Your talents could be put to use there instead of working with grubby children. You could teach gardening. I know how you love it so. I was appalled to know you were bunking with complete strangers. Honestly, I just don't know where I went wrong. Never fear, though. Whenever you tire of this adventure and rebellion you may come back home. We will get you squared away and back on track to become an influential member of this society. Just don't take too long, please. You are not getting any younger.

Loving always,
Your Mother

GLADYS HAD to laugh it off. This letter topped off the less than delightful afternoon she was having. Her mother would never get it. This was her work. This was not an adventure or rebellion. This was what she loved. Those grubby children were better company than any of those who ran in her mother's circles. She folded the letter up and stuffed it back into its envelope.

The trick with her mother was not to let her get under your skin. She had learned this technique a while ago and was now a master at implementing it, or so she hoped.

CHAPTER 6

$\mathcal{M}$icha Ulinski removed his hard hat and sat on his ladder-back chair. He wiped a grubby hand down his face as Lady, his mutt, came and nuzzled his other hand for a scratch.

"Oh, girl, I bet you're ready for some dinner. Let me get the fire going and wash up a bit and I'll get something together for you."

He stacked some dry kindling and a sliver of pitch wood beneath it into the fireplace, lit the match, and watched the flames come to life. Micha fiddled with it for a few moments to make sure it would take off before he padded over to his wash basin.

The water from this morning remained, but he didn't care. He dunked his hands in and scrubbed off what he could before moving to tackle his face. The water was a bit mucky to begin with, but after he finished, it was black. Coal dust settled on everything and when Micha got home it would transfer from him to every surface and every object in his home. Most days when he was deep in the mine, he could taste coal. Black was his world and he lived for his days off when he could feel the sun on his face.

He immigrated from Poland to the states several years before. His father's land had been taken from them, the same land that was one day to be his, his dream of a future with it. Without that land they had no way to provide. No future to continue growing the family.

Micha moved to gain employment to send funds back home. Finding work back East after he docked was challenging. Especially at first when he didn't speak the language very well. He had only ever known farming, making him not in demand for other jobs. So many people were moving to the West for a promise of opportunity and he followed suit. He missed Poland. He missed his family.

His Tato sent letters, but Micha couldn't read. Tato knew this, and he included drawings, so Micha could get an idea of what he'd written. It wasn't for lack of trying to learn to read. Many boys around him never learned. His Tato was adamant that he worked on it, but he just could not figure it out. The letters seemed to jump around on the page. His brothers and sisters learned, but he eventually gave up trying.

Micha placed a plate on the floor for Lady and sat down to eat his own cold meal. Mrs. Crowley had brought over some food the day before and he was still eating on it. There were a few of the married women who kept him and others going. He was thankful for that. He would love to settle down with someone, but so far that wasn't possible.

Mrs. Crowley did bring an exciting prospect with her when she brought the food. Having Miss Wimble come to regularly clean up would be nice. He didn't have much energy left when he returned home from work. It would dip into his low funds, what with him splitting them back home, but it would be a small comfort he hoped he could afford.

Knowing who it was shocked him a bit. After their first meeting he assumed she would never want anything more to do with him. She certainly seemed angry and uptight.

At first, he assumed that was just who she was, but thinking more on it led him to realize he was judging too quickly. It was her first day teaching in a new place and he, for one, knew what being new to the area meant. She probably had a mixture of nerves and fear running through her.

Micha decided to try to get to know her a bit more before he decided to judge her character. Besides, he didn't like when he was judged before anyone got to know him. And boy, had he experienced that several times since moving here. Being an immigrant, poor, and illiterate set many minds before he ever got to prove himself.

Micha cleaned his plate and Lady's before adding some bigger logs to a now glowing base of embers, then took a seat by the fire where Lady curled at his feet.

He pulled off his boots and used his foot to rub Lady's back while he pulled out his pocket knife and began whittling on a chunk of wood he'd picked up by the mill on his way home.

He liked to carve little animals. The mantel above the fireplace held his creations. He had created a dog as closely to Lady as he could get, a roe deer just like ones back home, a turtle, and was currently working on a bear. He kept them all up and out of Lady's reach when he was not working on them. He didn't want Lady to chew on them the way she tore into sticks she found and the occasional sock.

As he whittled, he thought about what he would ask Miss Wimble to do. There were many things he could put on the list, but some he was a bit uncomfortable asking. A laundry service currently took care of his wash. He thought he might keep it that way, so the teacher didn't need to see or handle his grubby clothes.

"I'm sure a young lady like herself would appreciate not dealing with my long johns," Micha told Lady who looked up at him and cocked her head to the side, ears perked.

Removing the coal from essentially every surface in the house could easily go on that list, though. He would be thankful to be able to touch things without needing to wash his hands. If only he could visit with her while she worked. He missed company. That was improper and he and Mrs. Crowley already discussed her working here while Micha was at work.

Knowing that someone else was here, even if it was not at the same time, would be a change. Having things taken care of by her would lend a bit of company in its own way. He wouldn't feel completely alone anymore. He could look around the room and see where she had been and what she had done.

Micha looked down at Lady. "Now, you are going to behave yourself while she is here working, right?" Micha sighed. He didn't like leaving Lady by herself while he worked, but he certainly couldn't take a dog into the belly of the earth.

Well, horses go down there.

The quiet was hard some nights. Back home, his house was always full. Quiet was a precious commodity. Here it was so quiet, if it weren't for the fire popping and crackling, he would think he'd gone deaf.

The work days were long, but these lonely nights seemed just as long for their own reasons. Night had fallen just minutes earlier and Micha decided it was late enough to finish up and head to bed. He was tired. At least in sleep he could let his dreams take him wherever his mind decided. He brushed the shavings from his lap into the fire and bid Lady good night as he lumbered off to bed.

CHAPTER 7

*G*ladys continued to work on a solution for her non-fluent English speaking students. Her only solid plan was to split lunch periods. Dividing the class up into two separate lunch breaks would give her time to focus on a smaller group and some students individually. It would also mean she wouldn't be able to have lunch. Until she could form a new, better plan it would have to do. She could eat her lunch in small amounts throughout the day.

After her meeting with Mr. Davis, she decided not to speak with the other teachers regarding their trip. Gladys hoped she simply slipped their minds or there was another decent reason for them not including her in their plans. But she couldn't shake the feeling that they didn't like her. She didn't know what she did to cause it. Thinking back over the few times she had been in their presence held no clues as to why they wouldn't like to spend time with her. Gladys had bigger issues though and needed to push that aside and focus on the more pressing matters, her students, for one, and moving for the second.

Her time at the Crowley home was coming to an end and she would be moving on to the next family's home. Sylvia had told her that they volunteered for another month in the rotation, but it would be several months yet before she was back with them.

Mr. Davis had already lined up multiple months in advance so not to allow for a period in which she overstayed, due to not having another in place.

Gladys had yet to be told of her next home. Despite the difficult sleeping arrangements, she would miss them. Sylvia was becoming a friend, or at least the closest to a real friend she had ever had.

Gladys finished rearranging the desks back into rows. The class had been working in groups before she dismissed them for the day. She was going to have the class set the room back to rights, but time had gotten away from her. As she moved the last desk back, tiny feet ran up behind her and little arms wrapped her in a hug at her hips.

"Hi, Gladys!" Sadie said while catching her breath.

Gladys gently freed herself, turned, and knelt. "Hello, Sadie. What are you doing back here? I just sent you home.

"Momma was on her way here to talk with you. I raced her and I won!"

Gladys chuckled. "I can see that." Sylvia was just making her way through the door. "Sadie, why don't you get yourself a ladle of water."

Sadie turned to do just that as Sylvia approached Gladys. "Hello dear. How was your day?'

"Oh, it went pretty well. I'm really enjoying the children. They are all wonderful."

Sylvia questioned that. "All of them?"

Both ladies chuckled. "Well, there are a couple of kids who like to test me from time to time, but I still really enjoy them. I may have the busiest age group in the school, but my kids love to learn and I try to make it fun, which helps, too."

Sadie piped up. "She is fun, Momma. We play games and sing songs."

Sylvia patted her daughter's head to quiet her down, "That's good. You really are a blessing and a great addition around here."

"Well, enough about me. What brings you here?"

Gladys tried to deflect the conversation. She wasn't used to genuine compliments and wasn't sure how to accept them graciously.

"Ah, the gentleman I talked to you about a while back is home today. I was hoping you would have time to pay him a visit, with me of course, to set up your new job."

Sylvia was fidgeting with her hands.

Gladys was confused by Sylvia's obvious nervousness.

Does she think I won't be able to do the work?

"I do have some time. I'm finished here. Let me grab my things and I'll meet you outside."

Sylvia led Sadie outside to wait for Gladys. All of a sudden she was nervous. Gladys didn't know why. It was just another job opportunity, a way to earn more money to hopefully get her into her own place sooner. She walked to her desk to pick up her things before looking the room over one last time to make sure everything was done for the day.

She met Sylvia and Sadie in the play yard. Sadie was in a swing and Sylvia was pushing her. "That looks fun!"

Sadie giggled. "It is. You should try it!"

Sylvia stopped pushing and let Sadie slow down on her own.

"I might try it one of these days, but for now I'll keep my feet on the ground." Gladys closed the remaining space and waited with Sylvia for Sadie to slow to a stop.

Sadie jumped when the swing slowed down a bit but perhaps still too early as she landed on her feet, but fell backwards.

"Oh Sadie! Are you all right?" Sylvia helped her back up.

"I'm okay, Momma. That was fun!" Sadie attempted to brush off her bum and Sylvia helped causing Sadie to turn red with embarrassment. "Momma!" She scolded and puffed her rosy cheeks.

"All right ladies, are we ready now?"

Sylvia grabbed Sadie's hand and the three of them took off down the dirt road. Other's on foot, in wagons, on horses, and even one horseless black carriage motored past them as they made their way to a very simple little home.

The yard was void of shrubbery and flowers. There were no clothes on the line. One might say it looked vacant.

Sylvia bent down to Sadie and instructed her to remain quiet while they were there. Sadie nodded in agreement as Sylvia then knocked on the heavy wooden door and it was immediately followed by a barking from within the home.

The unexpected noise startled Gladys and her heart raced. She could hear heavy footsteps approaching the entry. Before she could piece it together, the door opened, and a dog pounced out and began licking Sadie's face. Sadie, of course, was giggling between the dog's wet kisses.

Gladys looked up to see a tall lanky man standing before her, wiping his hands on a well-used hand towel.

"It's you!" Gladys gasped. She threw a hand over her mouth, instantly realizing she had not just thought the words.

CHAPTER 8

*M*icha knew who would be coming. He wasn't prepared for her attitude to start at the door though. Maybe this was a bad idea after all. He certainly didn't need this type of person in his life, even if he didn't have to spend actual time with her.

"Mrs. Crowley," he gave a nod and a smile. "Miss Wimble," a short nod only. "Please come in."

Gladys closed her eyes and took a deep breath.

"Mr. Ulinski, please accept my apologies for my behavior in the classroom. I was flustered and let it get the best of me."

Micha looked at her for a few moments, weighing her sincerity. "Apology accepted. I know I already apologized for my dog's behavior, but I truly am sorry. I don't know how or why she did that. Lady is normally very well behaved." He looked over at Lady and saw that she was enjoying getting attention from Sadie.

Sylvia's eyes darted between the two.

"Thank you. I have kept my eye out looking for you so I could make amends to the way I treated you." Gladys lowered her head and clasped her hands in front of her.

"Yes, well, Mr. Ulinski, this is who I spoke to you about. I see you two have already met." Sylvia gave a questioning look to Gladys. "If we could go over the duties expected and days that would work and then we will be on our way."

"Yes, of course. Please, come sit." he motioned to the table in the middle of the room and the three took a seat. "As you can see," he scanned the room with his eyes before settling on Gladys, "the house needs a good scrubbing."

"Yes, I can see that." Gladys face was pinched.

"If this is too much, I..." Micha began, but Gladys interrupted.

"No, it's fine."

"All right, then, I do appreciate this. I was hoping you could do the standard cleaning: floors, furniture, walls?"

Glady's eyes grew round and she looked around the room.

"Um, Okay."

Her words came out a bit shaky, an indication of how she felt, Micha assumed. He was thrilled with her 'okay' answer.

"Well, okay then. Now, I work Monday through Saturday for two weeks and then I have two days off in a row before going back to the regular schedule. That gives you several days to pick from to get this done. I know you teach Monday through Friday. There is some time after school lets out before I get home. Saturday is the only full day you would have without me here. I don't mind if you do all of the work in one day or if you would prefer to divide it up throughout the week."

"Do I need to decide right now? I'm going to be moving and would need to speak with my new boarders to see if they have a preference."

Gladys looked at Micha briefly, before turning to look at Sylvia.

"Of course. I really don't need to know either. I will give you a key and you can come and go as you please. I'll know if you've been here or not when I come home at the end of the day." Micha drummed his fingers on the table. "Now, for pay. I'll expect you to keep track of your hours. Since I won't be here, I'll have to trust you. I'm certain your math skills are gooder than mine."

"Ah, you meant to say..."

Sylvia cleared her throat and Gladys stopped mid-sentence.

"Well, sir, my hours are limited, so I will need to use my time well while I'm here."

"Good." He folded his hands in front of him on the table. "How about we try ten cents per hour worked?"

Gladys opened her mouth, but nothing came out.

"That will be just fine, Mr. Ulinski!" Sylvia interjected and gave a pointed look to Gladys.

"Yes, thank you."

Sylvia stood. "Well, we best be on our way. Come along, Sadie." At that point, Gladys stood, too, and followed Sylvia to the door.

The little girl didn't want to leave Lady. They were having a wonderful time playing with each other.

"Supper preparations are calling me. Thank you again, Mr. Ulinski, for this gracious opportunity. Gladys is a wonderful teacher and I'm hoping to do what we can to firmly plant her here to stay."

Gladys looked at Micha. "I do appreciate this. And I look forward to starting."

———⋎———

THEY PARTED, after Micha gave Gladys a key. The women and Sadie headed back to the Crowely's home. "Are you really appreciative Gladys?" Sylvia questioned her last comment to Micha.

"Yes, of course," Gladys immediately answered.

Sylvia stopped walking and placed a hand on her hip. "You could have fooled me."

"Oh, I'm trying," Gladys sighed. "It seems everything I say to that man is wrong. I am becoming afraid to speak to him."

Sylvia huffed and continued on with Sadie and Gladys following behind. Gladys knew this would be laborious work. She had never been tasked with this amount of labor before and hoped she had it in her to do it. She never knew walls would need scrubbed down before today. And so much dirt on everything was mind boggling. Gladys wondered if the home had ever been cleaned before.

"Just what is that black filth, anyway?" She attempted to wipe her hands to no avail. Not only was it dusty, but it clung to you like grease from the bacon pan.

"That black, my dear, is coal. It's what I clean every day. Once you get a handle on it, it's not so bad. Staying on-top of it is the best approach." Sylvia chuckled under her breath.

Huh, well that makes sense.

Gladys had seen men covered in black walking around town and she saw Mr. Crowley and Mr. Davis come home with black on them. The two homes she had been in had been kept very clean. She hadn't realized it would transfer. Ironically, that filth was an honest tale of hard work and income.

Back home, the filthy houses her mother pointed out were anything but well employed, but perhaps even then she had been too quick to judge. It seemed this teacher had much to learn. She just hoped she was up for the task.

CHAPTER 9

*G*ladys had spent the morning packing. Sadie was very sad to see her go, despite being reminded repeatedly that she would see her every day at school. Truth be told, Gladys was also sad to be leaving. She knew she could visit though. She was just moving a few houses over to the Kilpatrick residence.

Mr. and Mrs. Kilpatrick had four children, all sharing one room. The youngest child was in Gladys' class. The other three were older and in the other two classrooms. The house was tiny, and they were cramped. There was a pallet bed made up in the corner of the main room and Gladys discovered it was hers. She wouldn't be sharing a bed this time, but she also wouldn't have any sort of privacy.

"Your trunk can sit along the wall next to the bed.

You will be up by five and in bed by eight. We keep tight to those hours. Mr. Kilpatrick works long hours and needs plenty of rest," Mrs. Kilpatrick said with an Irish clip to her tongue.

"Yes, ma'am," Gladys replied, afraid to say any more.

"Momma runs a tight ship around here. Just stay in line and you'll be fine," a red headed blossoming girl who looked to be around sixteen whispered in Gladys' ear.

Gladys just nodded back. The warm, welcoming feeling from both places she stayed before was not found in these walls. She reminded herself that it was just for a month. She could do this, not that she had any choice in the matter.

"Meals will be served at six-thirty, noon on week- ends, and six. You will be required to help with preparations and clean-up except for the noon meal when you are working. During the week you will help with packing of the noon meals for the children and Mr. Kilpatrick. I take care of my own noon meal during the week. Washing the bedding will be a joint task between you and Sarah here," Mrs. Kilpatrick pointed to the red-head that had whispered to Gladys. "Sundays we will make the bread." She looked to them both.

Gladys was here to teach. She needed time to prepare for that. With the schedule laid out before her she was wasn't sure when she was going to have time.

"We have boarders from time to time and they all pay. You will not be paying, so your payment will come in the form of work."

"Yes, ma'am." Gladys was feeling like a child and uneasy about the situation. She wondered how she would manage to keep up with her work at the school, the work to do here, and the work at Mr. Ulinski's. She scanned the room. It was all hard. No frills. She couldn't help but think that this was going to be a very long month.

Besides Sarah, she met three boys: Cian, the eldest of the boys at fourteen, Tomas age ten, and Brin, who was a second-grade student in Gladys' class.

"Mrs. Kilpatrick?" Gladys needed to gain some confidence speaking to this woman.

She turned and looked Gladys in the eyes blinking in annoyance. "Yes."

"I, uh, well, I just thought, uh..."

"Out with it. I don't have all day now."

"Yes, ma'am, I have a job..." *No that's not right. She knows that.* "I mean, a second job, ma'am."

Mrs. Kilpatrick stood with her arms crossed and

her toe tapping the floor, "Yes, go on."

Gladys fiddled with the cuff of her sleeve. "I'm not sure how I will do both jobs and all the work that is required here."

"I see. Well, you could pay boarding fees if you wish. Then I would remove some of the chores from your schedule."

Oh, that wouldn't do. Gladys was trying to save money, not spend it. Especially not for a bed in the main room. "I need to do some scheduling is all. I will figure it out, ma'am."

Mrs. Kilpatrick looked her up and down. "See that you do. And for goodness sake, child, quit fiddling!" She turned on her heel and pushed through the back door leaving Gladys and Sarah alone in the room.

"Please, don't let Momma get to you. She is like that with everyone," Sarah tried to reassure her.

"I'll try to remember that." Gladys was stunned and wasn't entirely sure what she had gotten herself into.

"She can be softer, well, softer than what she was

just now. Especially once she gets to know you. She's had a rough life."

Gladys' life was rosy and she knew it. It didn't stop her from being down right mean to others. Her parents spoiled her, no doubt, and put her on a pedestal. Maybe this will be payback. "I'm sorry to hear that. I will do my best here and maybe we can become friends. Tell me about your class."

"Oh, it's normal, I guess. Miss Dupont can act like Momma at times. Some of the girls say she's like that because no man wants to marry her, and she is stuck teaching forever. I often wonder if she has had some troubles like Momma has."

Gladys really didn't want to get to know Miss Dupont now. Nor did she care to spend her off time with her. "What kind of troubles has Mrs. Kilpatrick had?" she softly pried.

"Well, life's just been all uphill for us. We came over on a big ship when I was about three. Cian was just a wee baby. Our daddy got real sick and died on the boat. Having no money and no way to turn around she married the first single man who'd take her. He's been okay. We have a home and food and I have two more brothers from it. I just don't know that he loves Momma. I really don't think Momma loves him either."

That was sad, indeed. Gladys hoped this young lady was still innocent enough to be naïve to such adult troubles and she hoped Sarah was either wrong or had exaggerated the situation. She would be able to figure it out living with them.

"Well, Sarah, we can't change the past, but maybe we can help make their future brighter. Of course, I want to get to know them a bit, but a little sincerity and some subtlety can go a long way."

"You can sure try, but no one has been able to crack her." Sarah stood with hands on hips emphasizing the point.

Gladys paused thinking about the situation. "Being nice is the only approach to take. If she treats me like this when I'm nice to her I can't imagine how she would treat me if I dished it right back." Both girls chuckled a bit. "You know, Sarah, I used to be cruel and malicious. I've changed. Or I hope I have. I still slip up from time to time. A bad habit is hard to break. For me it was learned behavior. I grew up with a mother who was the same." She looked up and nodded her head. "I'm proof people can change. What you are doesn't have to be what you will be." Gladys hoped she sounded sincere, as she was still battling with knowing that and believing it.

"Oh, well Miss Dupont says...oh never mind. She is just as bad as Momma."

Gladys wasn't sure she wanted to know what Miss Dupont said. She would tuck that information back and drop the subject for now. This was looking to not be an easy month and Gladys was glad she had an end date to focus on. She just wished the rest of this situation would get better. She had yet to feel like she was home and knew for certain the next thirty days wouldn't change that.

CHAPTER 10

*G*ladys moved through her week in a blur. She had little time to herself and found it easier to stay at school working longer than taking the work home as she had done in the past. If she wasn't there, Mrs. Kilpatrick couldn't find things for her to do. Gladys hoped that she wouldn't get upset with her for that. Mr. Davis hired her to teach, and so long as she was doing that, even if it was after hours, Mrs. Kilpatrick couldn't forbid her to stay. Finding time to clean for Mr. Ulinski was another problem she must figure out, and quickly.

Gladys wondered how Mr. Ulinski took up residence in the house. She had discovered through talks with the Kilpatrick children that all the single miners lived in the bunkhouse across the tracks. He was the only single man in his own home. The bunkhouse provided room and board for a fee. They didn't need to clean or cook. It seemed that would be a better set up for him.

After Gladys finished writing down the words to a few Christmas songs on the board that the children would be learning for their upcoming Christmas program, she decided to go straight from the school to Mr. Ulinski's home before going back to the Kilpatrick's home. She was fairly certain Mrs. Kilpatrick would be irritated that she wasn't there to help with the evening meal, but maybe if she didn't eat it, it would calm her a bit. She knew Mr. Ulinski would appreciate a hot meal and decided, despite it being part of her to do list, she could make a little more and eat there before he came home.

A soggy Lady ran up to her before she made it to the door. She gave her a pat and, after unlocking the door, the two of them made their way in. She found a lantern and used it to light up the dark corners of the home.

The next order of business was to start the fire. She wanted to heat the cleaning water before she began scrubbing. After the fire was roaring, Lady curled up in front of it, no doubt to dry off, which sent a wet dog smell permeating through the room.

Gladys began searching for rags or towels that she could use to clean. Mr. Ulinski hadn't explained where to find such things or how he wanted it done. Based on the filth surrounding her she wondered if he knew the answers to those questions.

She found a worn sheet in a cupboard and decided to rip it up for rags. Given that it already had tears here and there ripping wasn't a struggle. She found a bar of soap and tested the water temperature, which was tepid, but no longer cold. It would do. She began soaping up the rags and working on the furniture. She wanted to be able to sit and not ruin her dress or need to wash her hands afterwards.

After the table was washed up, she decided to put on a simple soup for supper. Broth would just be flavored from whatever she threw in and a little salt. He didn't have much stocked in the way of provisions. She did find some canned venison and assumed one of the married women gave it from their supplies. A bag of potatoes and some root vegetables were also found bundled in baggage from the company store. There wasn't time to make bread, but the soup would warm the belly and it was hearty enough it should hold them until breakfast. She just hoped the vegetables were fully cooked by the time she needed to eat.

After the soup was on, she discovered the dishes and utensils needed a scrub as well. He didn't have many, making that task go quickly. No two pieces seemed to match.

From the wash basin she raised her eyes to the remaining tasks. The walls would be next, but she was running out of clean rags and the soapy water was now black. She stepped outside to dump the water and start over when she realized the men were making their way back home. Time had gotten away from her and she needed to hurry. She wouldn't get to eat, but at least she took a chunk out of the cleaning here. Leaving Lady laying in front of the fire, she made her way outside so Mr. Ulinski and she wouldn't find themselves inside alone together. She waited for him in front of the house.

He was whistling as he walked home. "Hello, Miss Wimble."

"Mr. Ulinski." Gladys wanted to keep it short so she didn't end up saying something she would regret later.

"Are you just leaving?" Mr. Ulinski stopped a few paces in front of her. Lady could be heard tapping on the door and whimpering. Gladys let her out and she greeted her master with her tail wagging.

"I have more work to do, but since you are now home I must be on my way. I hope you don't mind, but I put soup on and kept the fire lit."

His eyes grew wide. "Don't mind? That is wonderful. I don't have hot meals regularly. Tonight, supper will be a treat."

"I'm glad you are okay with that. I really wasn't sure." Gladys remembered the rags that remained on the floor. "I also am hoping you don't mind that I used an old sheet for rags. It was already torn so I was thinking you wouldn't be too upset about that."

"No, that's just fine. I have a couple of rags I use to wash up dishes, but nothing for big cleaning."

Gladys looked back inside, realizing that the rags would need to be cleaned before she could work more. "If you'll stay out here for a moment, I'll go in and grab them to take with me. I will need to clean them up before next week."

Micha put his hand on the back of his neck, "You can if you want, but I can also just include them in my laundry. I have a laundress do it. She might charge me a little more, but I don't think it will be much."

Gladys sighed. She wasn't sure if she could add

them to the laundry that she was required to do or not. She already knew Mrs. Kilpatrick wasn't going to be pleased with her not being there today and didn't want to think of what adding more laundry would do to her mood. "That would be easier on me. Thank you."

"Not a problem. Would you like to be paid now or do you want to keep track and get paid monthly?"

Gladys knew being allowed to come weekly was hanging by a thread with her current living situation, "I would like very much to be paid now. Yes. Perhaps we can change arrangements when a routine is established."

Micha nodded, "I'll go get it. Just a moment."

He passed her and went inside. He took only a minute before he was back out, "How many hours have you been here today?"

Gladys thought back, she hadn't checked the time when she left school. "I honestly don't know. Not many, but I think it was somewhere between one and two."

"Well, it looks better already in there and you did get supper going for me. How about I pay you for two?"

Gladys didn't want to be paid more than she earned but couldn't remember for certain how long she'd been here. "If you think that's best, thank you."

Micha passed the coins to her and Gladys reluctantly headed for her current home. She was not ready to deal with Mrs. Kilpatrick, but knew she had to at some point. Now was just as good time as any. When she walked through the front door the family was sitting around the table eating. They all looked at her, the kids as if to say "you're gonna get it now."

"Where have you been, Miss Wimble?" Mrs. Kilpatrick put her fork down and waited for Gladys.

"Hello, I'm sorry I'm late. I stayed after at school to get some more work done and spent about an hour getting some of my cleaning job started."

"Well, since you missed your job here, you can either choose to not eat or pay for your portion of the meal." Mrs. Kilpatrick picked up her fork and began eating again. The children stared blankly at her and Mr. Kilpatrick, who sat opposite his wife, completely ignored the situation.

Gladys was hungry but refused to give up her hard-earned pay. She was already doing more here than she had at the other two homes. They understood she had more responsibilities and didn't require near as much from her. Gladys would just go hungry. Maybe instead of paying for her meal here she could go buy her meal from somewhere else so not to give Mrs. Kilpatrick the satisfaction.

"I'm more tired than hungry. I believe I will just head to bed early and rest up for tomorrow's work."

Mrs. Kilpatrick paused and stared at her. "Suit yourself, but don't get too comfortable. You will still be required to help with clean up."

Oh, the nerve! Gladys was really trying to like this woman. She knew something in her past must have made her this hard but being hungry and tired left no patience to deal with it.

"Yes, ma'am," Gladys said a little sharper than she intended to and Mrs. Kilpatrick stopped mid-bite and her eyes narrowed ever so slightly.

Gladys sat on her bed in the corner of the room waiting for the last of the children to finish eating. She was so mad she could spit nails. Using her frustration and the time to waste she grabbed a paper and pencil and wrote a letter to her mother telling her of her current living situation and her job cleaning. This would no doubt solicit a timely reply from her mother.

After the last person left the table, she and Sarah began work on cleaning it up. Mrs. Kilpatrick decided that since Gladys didn't help with preparations, she wouldn't help with clean up. That left just the two girls working together. It really didn't take long though and they were finished.

Gladys was truly tired from the day and decided to lay down. She wasn't sure if she could sleep through the noise of the family still being up, but her exhaustion from the long day of work proved stronger than the noises around her. She slept fully-dressed and on top of the covers, not caring at all.

CHAPTER 11

*G*ladys woke hours before the sun, just as she had every day since the first day she moved into the Kilpatrick home. Mrs. Kilpatrick was just starting the fire and Gladys and Sarah had only a few minutes to dress and ready themselves for the day before working together to make breakfast.

Sarah was putting on her apron when Gladys walked in. She handed Gladys her apron and went to collect the ingredients.

"What is for breakfast today?" Gladys was still groggy and used the back of her hand to rub the sleep out of her eyes.

"Black and white pudding," Sarah replied, setting

down oatmeal that had soaked overnight in water, salt, milk, pork fat, onion, spices, and blood.

Gladys looked over the food. "I'll tend to the coffee." She didn't mind the white pudding so much. It tasted more like oatmeal. She had yet to bring herself to try the black. There was too much blood in it, if any amount was acceptable. Gladys wasn't sure why it held the name pudding either. She thought, perhaps, it was due to the texture before cooking. After the milk was tempered to body heat the blood could then be added. Once those were mixed, every- thing could be incorporated before putting it all in a bread pan and baked. Gladys fried up some eggs with some wild mushrooms and onion. She preferred when they had the traditional Irish soda bread with jam.

"I was told to make extra and we will have it for supper," Sarah said as she was combining everything.

Gladys put her hand on her stomach, "Mm, good." She tried to sound genuinely glad for eating it twice in one day, but it came out sarcastically.

Sarah just laughed at her. "I think if you just tried the black pudding you would like it. It tastes like the white, but saltier."

That did not make her curious enough to try it. Gladys tried to not lose what little contents she had in her groaning stomach. "I'm good, but thank you. I'll just have to take your word for it."

"Suit yourself. It means more for us." Sarah formed the mush into the baking dish and set that to bake. She then went to set the table as Gladys finished up with the other dish.

Breakfast was eaten in silence. This was one of the family's favorite meals and talking took up eating time. Gladys watched them eat their "pudding" and thought maybe liking it was born into them. She didn't think she would ever get used to this food. Her eggs with mushrooms and onions were quite pleasing to the palate and filled her up well.

After breakfast was finished, the girls worked to clean up the mess and prep the lunches. Gladys then grabbed one of the lunches and flew out the door to arrive at school with just enough time to start the fire and fill the water pail. They would all need to wear their outer layers for a bit until the heat of the fire filled the room.

The children all gathered in and took their seats. Gladys smiled realizing with the kids wearing gloves they wouldn't be able to use their slates or books very easily. She decided to begin the day with the songs that she had written before. Plus having the kids stand and sing would help to warm them.

Gladys stood in front of the class and instructed them to stand.

"Class, as you know, we have a Christmas show to put on in a few weeks. That means we need to learn several songs. I have written the first three on the board behind me. Now let's begin by just reading the words. I would like my strong readers to make your voices heard so our non-readers can listen and follow along." Gladys scanned the class and noticed a few hands raised and many faces looking confused. "Do we have any questions before we start?" She called on one of the older girls, Helen, in the back.

Helen lowered her hand. "Miss Wimble, where are the words you want us to read? I don't see anything."

Gladys cocked her head to the side, "Well, they are just behind me." She turned and pointed to the board that was now wiped clean. She stood there a moment, confused at what she saw. She knew she had taken the time to write three songs down. Now they were gone. "What? How?" She turned back to the class. "I know I wrote them down. Did any of you erase them?"

After Gladys posed the question she realized how

absurd it sounded. The children just got here. They wouldn't have had the time to do that, especially without her noticing. All the children shook their heads no and a few said it out loud. There were only a few people who had access to the building and this room. She could see no reason why Mr. Davis would do this which left two others with access, the teachers.

Gladys closed her eyes and pinched the bridge of her nose. She pushed the thoughts aside and realized she had several young eyes looking at her that were waiting for direction. Gladys decided to push all of this aside and move forward as best she could through the rest of this practice.

"All right class, we will do this a different way. I will say a few words and you can repeat after me." She scanned the room and all heads were either nodding in agreement or silently awaiting to comply. She began by saying the first line in "The First Noel." Then the kids did their part. This went back and forth until they got to the chorus, where she then repeated the whole first verse again. Over-all, the children seemed to pick it up easily and many of them already knew the song.

After a while they had a good start on the first song and she decided to move on for the day. The room was warming nicely and she allowed the children to remove their outer layers. This allowed for regular instruction to begin. Thankfully the day ran smoothly once they overcame the earlier obstacle.

She had thought about approaching the teachers during lunch, but since she split the time to work on English she didn't have any time left to do that. By the end of the day she was glad she had not tried to. Most likely the teachers wouldn't have admitted anything anyway. Honestly, Gladys was trying her best to rationalize another suspect, but it was not seeming plausible.

Before class finished, she pulled a young boy aside, Freidrich, and asked if he would speak to his mother for her. She wanted the words to "O Tannenbaum" in German and knew the family spoke German. She wasn't sure if they would be willing to help her, but she certainly hoped so. Doing what she could to embrace the many countries represented in this small town was hopefully a way to work towards acceptance. She had yet to figure out ways to incorporate more, but was actively working on the task.

Gladys' schedule wouldn't allow for social or work visits beyond what she was already doing. She hoped his mother could come during school hours and write it down for her. If not, maybe one of the older children could help if their teacher allowed them to come meet with her.

Gladys dismissed the children and used her time after school to re-write the songs on the board. This time she decided to stay until she was the last to leave. At least she could lock everything up and know for sure no one but those three could enter until the morning.

She made her way back to the Kilpatrick home and dug right into work. Supper was not something she was especially looking forward to, given her knowledge of what was being served from breakfast. Leftovers did allow for some rare down time, however. Gladys pulled out her special items she brought from Deer Lodge and was arranging them on her bed when Sarah came over.

"Hello, Miss Wimble. What are those?" She sat at the foot of the bed looking at the contents spread before her.

Gladys had multiple bags of seeds and bulbs each labeled from a different flower. "These, my dear Sarah, are what will bring hope and beauty to this community."

Sarah's eyes narrowed, and her nose scrunched in confusion.

Gladys giggled. "They are seeds from my mother's garden," she added. "I'm planning on having the children plant some in a couple of months. They will grow indoors and then in the late spring we will take them to our homes and plant them in the yards. There are some flowers here and there, but most of this town is dirt."

Sarah smiled. "What will you do with the others?"

Personally, I will be planting some around the school and at a few homes here and there. I am saving some as well for my future home. My mother has the best garden. I used to work in it. I learned everything I know about plants and gardening there." Gladys closed her eyes and smiled remembering the joy from the roses in every color imaginable.

"It sounds lovely." Sarah's eyes sparkled with excitement.

Gladys opened her eyes and stared at Sarah. "Do you know anything about my boards being erased?"

Sarah cocked her head to the side and held a puzzled look on her face. "No, I don't think so. Why?"

Gladys paused, thinking over a response, but decided it was better to not mention it. "It's nothing. Forget I said anything." She didn't want Sarah going back to school talking about it and tipping off Miss Dupont. Gladys wasn't sure what to do from here but thought maybe if she pushed it off and forgot about it, whoever did it would think it wasn't a big deal.

"Here, help me sort these please. I'm grouping them based on bloom times. It's written on the sack." She was hoping changing the subject would distract her and Sarah would forget all about it. At least for the moment the trick seemed to work and the girls finished the task before Gladys put them away, now sorted.

Gladys worked the rest of the evening to focus on the here and now. Fretting over who might have done what solved nothing and only upset her more. She would keep her ears and eyes open but wouldn't go intentionally poking around for information.

CHAPTER 12

*G*ladys made it through the week without another incident. She was grateful for that, but she had yet to determine who or how it was done. After school she headed back over to clean more at Mr. Ulinski's. This time she didn't stay after school first, making her arrive at the Kilpatrick's earlier than before. She needed to be back in plenty of time to prepare and eat supper.

She entered the home with Lady on her heels and got right to work. Today she would not make supper for him in order to maximize what of her to do list she could accomplish and still make it back in time to avoid any issues. She prepared the water and began work where she had left off. Some of the grub that she cleaned off last week had started to collect again, but it wasn't as bad and took less time to rid it from its hold. She hadn't been working long before a knock sounded at the door. Gladys wasn't sure if she should open it or ignore it. This wasn't her home. When the knock came again, she decided to go ahead and see who it was. She could let them know Mr. Ulinski wasn't available at least. Upon opening the door, however, she found Sylvia smiling back at her.

"Hi, Gladys. I thought I might find you here since you weren't at the school. Actually, I hoped I would." Gladys gave Sylvia a hug and welcomed her in like it was her home. "Oh, it's so good to see you!" "It's really good to see you. I've missed you." Gladys pulled out a chair and sat, motioning her to do the same.

"Well, you know where I am. I don't want to bug you since I know you're pretty busy as it is, but you can always come find me when you have free time." She sat and noticed the table was now clean.

Gladys laughed. "When I have time? I never have time. Mrs. Kilpatrick has made sure of that." Gladys put her elbows on the table and placed her chin in her hands in a very improper fashion.

Sylvia's forehead wrinkled with concern. "Is she

working you too hard? I should have forewarned you. I wish Mr. Davis never allowed her to be in the rotation."

Gladys sighed. "She usually has paid boarders. I am paying in another way, but I'll be all right. I'm already half way through. And I've learned to just keep quiet and do the work and she doesn't bother me much."

Sylvia put her hand on Gladys' arm. "I'm so sorry, dear. Like you said, you are half way done. You'll be moving on before you know it." Gladys nodded in agreement. "Now, just look at this place. There is still much to do, but it already looks better. I can sit here and not feel I need to wash afterwards."

"Yes, the situation is improving, that's for sure." Gladys paused and thought for a moment before continuing, "Can I ask you something?"

"Of course, anything."

With a confused look on her face she placed her hands in her lap before jumping in. "Well, it's just that Mr. Ulinski lives here alone. He isn't married and hasn't been as far as I can figure. Why isn't he in the bunkhouse with the rest of the single men?"

Sylvia stood and walked over to Lady. "Well, the answer to that is right here." She patted Lady's head. "She doesn't like men. Mr. Ulinski is the only one she does. She barks at all others. No one knows why, but she does. He was in the bunkhouse, but too many other men complained. He was told to either move out or give up Lady. He refused, of course, claiming she was all he had and that was that. Lucky for him this house was vacant. They will boot him if someone marries or a married couple moves into town of course, but for now he is allowed."

Gladys looked down at Lady who was happily receiving the pats to her head by Sylvia. "Huh. So, he isn't allowed to take his meals there then? I only ask because he has very little food here."

Sylvia went back and sat down in the chair she occupied before. "He could if he wanted to. I guess he is still upset they made him choose. There is a small group of us married women who cook up extra and help him out for now while he figures out what to do next." She looked at Gladys out the side of her eye and added. "We are hoping to see him married soon."

Gladys looked Sylvia in the eyes, "He is interested in someone? I haven't noticed any female presence here," she said as she wiped a finger along the mantel.

Sylvia chuckled. "No, you wouldn't. It wouldn't be proper. I don't know if he does have any one. We just have our hopes. He is such a nice man. He just needs a female to help even out his edges and work on the home front. It would secure this as his home."

Gladys nodded. She understood, but hoped they weren't going to the levels her mother would have in order to play matchmaker. Sylvia was a different person, though, and she didn't want to be too quick to judge the situation. "I best get back to work. I can't stay much longer, or I'll end up missing supper again."

"Did she withhold food from you?" Sylvia was appalled.

Gladys pursed her lips to the side. "Well, technically no. She did allow me the option to pay for it since I didn't work for it."

Sylvia's jaw dropped. "The nerve. That woman, I swear. If that happens again you come find me. I will feed you. You are doing so much for this community and our children. The least we can do is make sure you don't go hungry and have a roof over your head."

Gladys smiled and hugged Sylvia. She thanked her and then showed her out so she could continue with her work. She wouldn't be around when Mr. Ulinski came home today, which meant she wouldn't get paid. She thought that was better than waiting and dealing with Mrs. Kilpatrick. She knew he would square up with her soon anyway.

Gladys hurried through to finish early enough to allow time to prepare dinner. She was happy with how the house was coming along and couldn't help but think of ways to decorate it. She knew she shouldn't, but ideas just kept popping into her head: angling the table to make the room look bigger, adding a few decorative pillows with pops of color perhaps in a floral pattern, or hanging some artwork on the walls. She shoved them aside as best she could and headed for her current residence.

CHAPTER 13

"$\mathcal{M}$ iss Wimble?"

"Yes, Sadie?" Gladys looked down at the sweet little girl that stole her heart.

"Henry tugged on my braid and called me a bonehead." Despite the look of hurt she held on her face she could tell by the twist of her foot Sadie was pleased that Henry would be getting into trouble.

"Henry, could you come here, please?" Henry and Sadie were assigned partners for reading today. Henry was older and a solid reader where Sadie was an emerging reader. He was supposed to be helping her sound out the words.

Henry slowly walked up with his hands in his pockets as the rest of the class began whispering.

"Yes, ma'am," he said while putting on his best bewildered face.

Gladys sighed. "Class, please focus on your work." She turned her attention back to the two children in front of her after the rest of the class settled back into their books.

"Henry, did you call Sadie..." She looked down at her and noticed Sadie was grinning from ear to ear. Gladys gave her a stern look, indicating to straighten up before continuing. "Did you call Sadie a bonehead?"

Henry, hands still in pockets, shuffled a foot on the floor and smirked a bit. "Yes ma'am."

"Did you also pull her braid?" Gladys added, already knowing the answer.

"Yes, ma'am." He kept his eyes on the ground.

Gladys turned to Sadie. "Thank you, Sadie. That will be all." She dismissed her back to her chair and Sadie sulked away wishing she could stay. She turned back to Henry. "Henry, why would you do that?"

The boy just shrugged his shoulders. His smirk was gone.

"Tell me what was going on before you did this."

He looked up at her. "She was trying to sound out

the same word we already went over before and she couldn't remember it."

Gladys understood now. "You lost your patience. You thought she should know it and when she didn't you got frustrated."

He nodded.

"Henry, I want you to think about something. Have you always known how to read?"

Henry shook his head no.

"Did someone sit with you and help you learn?" She prodded on.

"Yes, ma'am, my older sister helped me."

"All right, then. Was she patient with you or did she get frustrated too?"

"Well, she was all right, I suppose. She never got mad at me." He wiggled where he stood ready to be done being in the hot seat.

Gladys paused and looked him over, "I want you to remember that. I'm sure you had words you stumbled over. Learning to read doesn't happen all in one day. It takes time. The most important part of learning to read is making sure the teacher keeps it positive. If the student feels like a failure, they will become a failure."

The boy looked up hopeful at Gladys. "I'm a teacher?"

Gladys chuckled. "Yes, you are a teacher. At least while you are teaching Sadie to read. If you call her names and pull her hair you are only an older boy picking on a little kid."

Henry smiled. "I never thought of it like I was teaching her. I'll do better, I promise."

"Good boy, Henry. Now, you go on back and teach your student." She put her hand on his shoulder and gave him an approving pat.

"Yes, ma'am!"

Gladys turned back around with a smile plastered on her face. She truly loved this age group. When Gladys was in the middle of writing the rest of the lyrics to another song down, she heard a knock on the door and the children turned to see who it was. Mr. Davis stepped in and approached Gladys.

"I don't mean to eavesdrop, but I was standing there for a while and saw how you handled that situation."

"You did?" Gladys' face flushed.

Mr. Davis smirked. "Yes, don't worry. You did well. I was impressed. You not only took care of it, but you did it with sympathy and teaching instead of reprimanding. Most teachers would have just put him in the corner for it. Well done, Miss Wimble. Well done."

Gladys beamed at the praise. Then he pulled out an envelope and her heart sunk. She knew one would be coming. She had sent her letter that she wrote when she was angry with Mrs. Kilpatrick off fully knowing of what was to come.

"I don't want to take any more of your time, but this letter came for you and I wanted to make sure you got it."

She took the letter from him and thanked him. Gladys did not want to take the time to read it right now. She set it on her desk and continued with her day and her joys.

Unfortunately, the day had to come to an end. Gladys dismissed the children and sat at her desk looking at the envelope.

Better get it over with.

She ripped the seal and pulled out the paper.

GLADYS DEAR,

I was shocked and angered when I read your letter. How dare she not feed you! And what is this about you cleaning house for an unmarried man?

You are lowering yourself to a commoner. We are not common, dear. Please, think about what you are doing. Now, if you need money, I can send it to you. We can pay for your lodging. Although, just giving up this hairbrained idea and moving back home would be best. My groups keep asking about you and I was just twisting the truth, but now I am downright lying to save face, dear. You are shaming us. Teaching is one level, but cleaning? Oh, I cannot even imagine it. You correct this, or I will make my way out there and correct it myself.

Your mother, and don't you forget it.

Gladys sighed and stuffed away the envelope. She needed to remember her mother was not her friend. She shouldn't be so forth coming with her. Gladys tried to push her mother's words out of her mind as she worked to finish her day. Sometimes, most of the time, that was easier said than done.

CHAPTER 14

*G*ladys had been walking door-to-door asking for ideas for her Christmas project. Many of the residents of Ravensdale loved the idea and agreed to contribute. She had discovered many different countries had a whole special meal they served. Several homes offered to contribute a food, but since this program was an evening affair meant to happen after everyone supped, she decided just desserts would be best. Everyone could eat supper beforehand and together they could enjoy treats from around the world. A couple of ladies agreed to make and serve a beverage from their home country.

Fredrick was able to have his mother write the words down to "O Tannenbaum." Gladys was grateful for that. She knew she needed more though.

One song mixed with all American songs would stand out too much. She wanted more of a mix. She decided to walk in the direction of the Davis' home. She planned to let Mr. Davis know everything that she had pulled together, and he could then pass it along to the other two teachers. She wasn't ready to approach them.

"Hello, Miss Wimble."

Gladys turned to see who was speaking to her. She spotted Mr. Ulinski walking towards her. "Oh, hello, Mr. Ulinski. How are you?"

He closed the distance between them. "I'm doing good."

"Well, you are...oh, never mind." Gladys clamped her mouth shut.

Micha blew on his hands. "Mighty cold out today. What brings you out in the weather?"

"Yes, it sure is. I'm working on the Christmas pageant. I'm going to different homes and seeing if they might contribute."

"Well, I'd sure love to help if I can."

Gladys thought about that. He didn't have children in school, but that didn't mean he wouldn't attend the event. "We are singing songs and there will be food and drink. I wanted to make it extra special for those who might miss their home. I'm asking for ideas and help to bring something from a country that they come from." Gladys started walking again and Micha followed her. "So far we have different desserts and a couple of drinks, oh and there is one song from Germany."

"I can suggest another." He looked expectantly toward her.

"You can? Well, that would be terrific. I was hoping for more music."

"We have a few songs back home. One of my favorites is "Bóg Się Rodzi." It means God is born."

Gladys smiled, "Well that sounds lovely. Do you think you could write the words down and help me learn the melody of it?"

Micha paused and put his hand on the back of his neck. "Oh, uh, ya I guess."

"Oh, that's just wonderful! I would need it soon, so the kids could have enough time to learn it, of course. Say, why don't you just leave it on the table and I can grab it next time I'm there?" Gladys was talking very quickly now, excited for the addition.

"Uh, sure."

"Oh, and maybe if you can pop in during school, you could help us learn the melody. Thank you so much. I'm off to speak with Mr. Davis. It was a pleasure to see you." Gladys almost skipped all the way she was so happy.

Mr. Davis' home was not far from where Gladys and Micha separated. She knocked on the door and waited.

Mrs. Davis opened the door. "Oh, hello dear. What brings you by?"

"Hi, Mrs. Davis. I was hoping to speak with Mr. Davis. Is he available?"

Mrs. Davis nodded her head. "Yes. Do come in, please. I'll let him know you are here."

"Thank you."

Mrs. Davis left the room and returned moments later with Mr. Davis. "Hello, Miss Wimble. What can I do for you? Everything is fine at the school, yes?"

"Yes, oh yes, I'm sorry to disturb you. I was hoping to go over some plans with you." She bit her bottom lip.

"Of course, please come, sit down." He gestured towards a chair.

They both took their seats before she continued. "As you know, we have a Christmas program coming up. I have been working with the children on learning songs to sing. It's going very well."

"That is great to hear. I love the program and the

kids always have fun with it. I know this will be your first, but don't be nervous please. It is just a great night to get together and celebrate."

"Oh no, I'm not nervous." She paused before plowing ahead, "I had this big idea to incorporate as many different countries as possible by having someone in the community from another country contribute a song from their Christmas celebration."

Mr. Davis paused, and a grin grew on his face. "Well, that sounds like a great idea. This little town holds people from all over the world. I'm sure finding what you are looking for hasn't been diffi-cult. Do you need me to ask around though? Are you struggling to pull enough together?"

"Oh no. I have a great start on that. The issue is that my portion is only the music. The other teachers have decoration and refreshments. It seems that most of the families would like to provide in their categories rather than mine. It seems I have already done most of their work for them and I'm worried how they will take the news."

"I see," he nodded his head and folded his hands while tapping his thumbs together. "Well, I like the idea and think we should follow through with this. Why don't I speak with the other two?"

"Would you? That would be wonderful." She exhaled loudly.

Mr. Davis chuckled. "Of course I will. Don't you worry about those two. They are good teachers if you get to know them."

"Thank you for speaking with them. I do hope this doesn't cause any issues."

They stood and Mr. Davis walked her to the door, "I'm sure of it. If anything, you saved them work. I bet they are thankful to you for stepping up and reducing their load."

Gladys was certain that wouldn't be the case but didn't want to argue. "Thank you, again, Mr. Davis. I'll be on my way now."

"Sure thing, Gladys, anytime." Mr. Davis closed the door as Gladys walked back to where she came.

CHAPTER 15

*G*ladys had a rough start to the day after she'd somehow slept in and no one bothered to wake her. Once she did rise, Mrs. Kilpatrick expected her to still attend to her morning work before she could make her way through the rain to the school.

Fortunately, besides one hiccup where Miss Siller glared at her from down the hall due to the students making too much noise and not being able to find her broom, the day went off without another hitch and she walked back to the Kilpatrick residence in dry conditions.

Gladys no longer took Mrs. Kilpatrick's harsh firmness personal. She learned that the woman treated everyone the same. Gladys felt a bit sorry for her. No one came to visit. She wasn't involved like her mother was back in Deer Lodge. She really had nothing outside of her family and their home.

Gladys walked through the door and set her things down on her trunk. She then grabbed her work dress, changed into it, and set out to scrub the floors. As she reached the bedroom where she could change in private, she heard voices. She paused not wanting to interrupt whoever was in there, but unsure of where else she could go to change. Gladys listened to see if she could judge whether she could knock on the door or if waiting for a while was better. The voices that came back to her were those of the children. That relaxed her a bit. At least it wasn't Mrs. Kilpatrick. She would have wanted her changed and working by the time she saw Gladys but wouldn't have wanted her to interrupt to do so. Gladys raised her fist to the door as she heard her name pass from Sarah's mouth. Her hand hovered in midair as she listened to what came next.

"Miss Wimble apparently planned the whole thing and Miss Dupont was none too happy about it either." Gladys lowered her fist, but kept listening. "My class was working on coming up with the refreshment ideas. We had formed groups and each group was to prepare one item," Sarah continued.

One of the boy's voices could be heard next, but Gladys couldn't make out which one. The two younger boys sounded identical. "Ya, and we were making paper chains and pictures to decorate. Miss Siller had more plans, too, but she hadn't told us yet."

Ah, it was the older of the two youngest Kilpatrick children, Thomas. Gladys wanted to keep listening, but knew it was wrong to eavesdrop. When she had the idea to talk to the community, she was thinking about entertainment ideas, which was her area. When people started offering the other, she didn't want to be rude and reject it. She knew there might be some hurt feelings, which was why she went to Mr. Davis asking to break the news. She hadn't realized that the other classes would have already been in full planning mode. She should have known. Gladys wasn't sure why that hadn't dawned on her.

"Miss Siller says that Miss Wimble moved here because she had to." Gladys leaned in more. "Something about losing her job in Montana because she was caught keeping mixed company."

Gladys sucked in breath rapidly and stumbled backwards. She left Montana on her own terms. Never had she ever broken any of the teaching codes.

How dare she!

She held on to the back of the chair she had stumbled back into. Gladys was struggling to breathe. She needed air.

Dropping her dress on the floor she fled from the house and into the street. Her eyes were looking, but she wasn't seeing. She was blindly wandering, not caring where she went. Her reputation was impeccable.

Reputation was a funny thing. Her mother drilled it into her head. Building and maintaining your reputation took years, but losing it could happen in one second. One wrong move. Being in the wrong place at the wrong time. Talking to the wrong person. Everything a person worked so hard for could be gone in the blink of an eye. Tears began pooling in her eyes and leaving trails down her cheeks.

I haven't done anything.

She continued mindlessly walking until she found herself in front of a door. Gladys took a moment to get her bearings on her surroundings. Realizing finally where she was, she knocked. Footsteps sounded from the other side before the door creaked open. Gladys fell into the arms of the woman on the other side of the threshold and began sobbing.

"Oh dear. Oh, Gladys. What's wrong, dear?" Sylvia stroked her hair.

Gladys tried to inhale to get oxygen in order to talk, but was struggling to have any coherent sound escape.

"Shh, shh, it's all right dear. Whatever has happened, we can fix it." She backed up and moved Gladys into the house. Sadie walked into the room and paused staring. "Sadie, dear, will you please go bring us some tea?"

Sadie looked at Sylvia with big round eyes. "Momma? What's wrong with Miss Wimble?"

Sylvia shot her the look. "Never mind, Sadie. She is going to be just fine. The tea now, please."

Sadie's mouth was now gaping open and she slowly nodded her head before creeping out of the room.

Sylvia held Gladys and let her cry. She rubbed her back and spoke soft soothing words to try to comfort.

After several minutes, Gladys pulled back and took a few big hitched gulps of air while using her skirt to dab at her face. "I'm sorry. I don't know how I got here. I was at the Kilpatrick's and remember needing to leave, but I don't remember coming here."

"Did Mrs. Kilpatrick do something dear?"

Gladys put her fist in front of her mouth and shook her head no. "No, no. She doesn't know where I am. I haven't seen her since breakfast."

Sylvia's brows drew in concern. "What has happened?"

Gladys couldn't say the words. She was still trying to understand them herself. "I just don't know why someone doesn't like me."

"Who doesn't like you?"

Gladys' eyes grew large, "Oh no. I was on the reverse. That was me. No, talking about this is going to make it worse."

Sylvia blinked a few times. "Gladys, I do not know what you are talking about. You are not making any sense."

Gladys started looking around the room. "Oh, I'm sorry. I... I need to go." She fled from the house as Sadie entered, bringing the tea leaving them both staring at the door.

CHAPTER 16

Gladys knew Sylvia would be wondering what that was all about. She should have either told her everything or never went in the first place. The problem was she wasn't sure if she could trust her. She didn't know who she could trust.

Gladys knew the game Miss Siller was playing. Gladys had played it often herself. She never fully understood what her actions did to the other person but she was feeling it now. If this rumor started circling with the adults she could end up losing her job. Gladys was still new. She hadn't been here long enough to form a reputation. And with no one wanting to spend any real time with her, the prospect of beginning to form a genuine one was bleak.

One thing Gladys knew was if she didn't talk to Sylvia and give her something, most likely, Sylvia would come find her to get answers. Not knowing if Sylvia would keep her words to herself or not, Gladys thought up an explanation that she wouldn't mind if it got out. She wouldn't lie, but she certainly wouldn't share the whole truth.

After compiling what she thought would be enough to settle Sylvia, but not enough that could deepen the issue between her and Miss Siller, she found herself back on the Crowley's stoop. This would be a tough conversation, but she needed to have it.

Sylvia answered the door on the second knock. She was clearly surprised to see Gladys return so soon. The ladies sat at the table and Sadie brought the tea before Gladys began.

"I'm very sorry for coming in hysterical before and leaving without explanation." Gladys was much more composed this time.

Sylvia had her hands wrapped around her mug. "Don't apologize, dear. We all get emotional from time to time and I'm glad you came to me. I would like to help you if I can. I need to know what is going on first, though, to do that."

Gladys nodded, folded her hands in her lap, and lowered her head. "I've never moved before. I lived my whole life in the same town. Friends were built in growing up. I didn't have to figure out how to make them. And I certainly haven't had to do it on my own. My mother was always there to do it for me."

Sylvia cocked her head to the side. "I'm not sure why that should have upset you that much."

Gladys should have known she would need to go a bit farther to satisfy Sylvia. "I think my skin has worn thin with living with the Kilpatrick's and dealing with Mrs. Kilpatrick, on top of not having made any significant connections to anyone here, aside from you, of course."

She didn't want Sylvia upset with her, thinking that she didn't consider her a friend. And she was her only friend here, but it wasn't the same. She wanted someone or something like her friends from home. Well, maybe some of her friends from home. She would be fine never talking to a few of them again since she made a change in her life to be a better person than before.

Sylvia put her hand on the table in front of Gladys. "I think I know what's going on here."

Gladys' eyebrows shot up. "You do?"

"Of course, I do," she paused and gave her a small smile, "It's the holidays. You miss your family. I'm sure this time of year was special to you. You probably have routines and traditions that you are used to and all of that is changing this year. Everything is new."

Gladys released a breath she was holding and nodded. She supposed Sylvia was right in that. She may or may not have been as upset any other time of the year, but she did believe that this season was contributing to her loneliness she felt.

"Gladys, do you read your Bible much?" Sylvia stood and walked over to where hers was placed on the mantel. She thumbed through until she found what she was looking for.

"Not as much as I should," she visibly sank a bit. Gladys didn't really read it at all. Her mother started her attending church, so they could be seen, she figured, in their best clothes and fancy Sunday hats.

Sylvia set the Bible down on the table in front of her and pointed to a spot within. "This is Psalm 68: 5- 6. Please read it."

Gladys obliged. "I'm not sure what it means. I'm not fatherless, a widow, or a prisoner."

Sylvia laughed a bit. "Oh, Gladys. No, you are not technically any of those things, but you are alone right now. All those people that are named there are also alone. What does God say he does with the lonely?"

Gladys looked back down at the verse. "He sets them with families."

"Yes, dear. I believe God put you in my life to help. We are a family and you are lonely. I also believe that there will be more that will become family to you around here. It just takes time." Sylvia thought, but didn't speak about her hopes of Gladys and Micha becoming closer. "This year is rough, but you have me. You have us."

Sadie chimed in from the background, "You have me, Miss Wimble. I love you."

"Sadie, how long have you been there?" Sylvia turned and put her hands on her hips.

Sadie's eyes grew big, "Not long, Momma. I promise. I'm sorry. I'll leave now." She ran from the room.

Sylvia shook her head. "I'm sorry Sadie was eavesdropping. That child. She has a good heart, she just can be incorrigible at times."

Both ladies chuckled. "She is a good girl, Sylvia. You are doing a great job with her."

"Thank you. It's good to hear it even if I don't always believe it." Sylvia shook her head side to side with her eyes looking up at the ceiling. "So, back to you," she gave a pointed look towards Gladys. "This Christmas you will be celebrating here with us."

"Oh, I couldn't impose like that," Gladys interrupted.

"Nonsense. You are not imposing if you are invited. Now I'm not sure where you will be living next, but you should be finding out quickly."

Gladys nodded. "Yes, the move will be this next weekend. I'm assuming Mr. Davis will tell me any day now."

"Good." Sylvia nodded her head once. "You know you can always come here and talk with me, right?"

Gladys nodded. "Thank you for that. For being a friend. I'm not sure when I will have another."

Sylvia tipped her head side to side. "Well, you should be able to meet some at the Christmas program. Oh, and the baseball games."

"What?" Gladys hadn't heard about any games before.

"Oh yes, the games. They are big around here.

Each neighboring town has a team and they all compete against each other."

Gladys scrunched her nose. "The kids do? They haven't mentioned anything about it."

Sylvia shook her head no. "Well, the kids do play a bit, but these teams are formed from the grown men. It's a riot. They play as soon as the weather warms up a bit in the spring."

"Now that I'll have to see." Gladys wondered which of the men were on the team. She could be sneaky and ask the kids about it. See if they would know.

"I think part of the reason you haven't been able to make friends yet is just because you don't have much free time."

Gladys thought that was plausible. She wouldn't be making friends with the two most likely candidates, the other teachers, but she wasn't going to tell that to Sylvia.

"Thank you. You have made me feel a bit better. I had an idea of how moving here would go and it hasn't been lining up. I may be too antsy. I should let it take the time it needs." Gladys stood to leave.

Sylvia hugged her. "I'm glad you came back and talked with me. I'm always right here whenever you need to talk."

After they parted and the door closed, Gladys walked back to the Kilpatrick's and thought about what Sylvia said. It could be that she was judging the whole town from two people's actions.

Gladys wasn't friends with everyone back home. She didn't need to be friends or to be friendly to them. So long as they didn't ruin her reputation before she had a chance to make it, she would be fine. She needed to be careful. Gladys knew from experience that she couldn't give them an inch to go from. She had to stay squeaky clean so if they did try to run her through the mud she had proof it was all lies. Feeling more confident in her place in a long while she walked back into the Kilpatrick's with her head held high.

"Hello, Gladys." Sarah greeted her first.

"Hello, Sarah."

Sarah walked closer to her. "I found your dress on

the floor over there," she pointed, "I set it on your bed for you."

Gladys hesitated. "Thank you." She hoped Sarah wouldn't ask why it was there.

Sarah just looked sideways at her for a moment and then walked away. Gladys was thankful. She would not let on that she overheard anything. The less anyone knew of what she knew the better. Besides, if the kids are talking with each other here about it, they would be talking elsewhere to others. Hopefully, the rumor wouldn't find its way back to Mr. Davis. He would be required to follow up in some fashion on that. She inwardly groaned at the very idea of the conversation.

CHAPTER 17

*T*he week passed, and Gladys learned nothing more regarding the rumors she'd heard from the Kilpatrick children. She hoped that it meant it had already passed and nothing was to come of it. The other teachers didn't know anything about her past.

Gladys wondered how much trouble they could cause when it was obvious that only Mr. Davis knew anything regarding her history. She had an impeccable record and always stayed in good standing within the community. Her mother would have expected no less whether she liked it or not.

Growing up, Gladys had observed the other girls in her class. When they were little everyone seemed the same to her. She hadn't recognized the subtle differences. She only knew she wasn't allowed to associate with some. As she grew, she noticed what set them apart: worn or patched clothing, hand-me-downs, shoes that were too tight. For many years she felt above them.

She was always dressed in the latest fashions from back East, her hair done just so every day. As the years moved on, it seemed those girls she excluded were happier. They would always be seen together laughing and enjoying themselves. She and her friends would spend their time making derogatory comments about them or coming up with new ideas on how to snag the elite boys. Gladys knew her mother would expect her to stay the course she set for her. It didn't mean she had to like it.

Telling her mother she would rather teach than marry was one of the hardest things she had ever faced. It was the first time she'd stood up to her and spoke her own mind. She knew ahead of time what her mother's reaction would be. She wasn't prepared for her father's.

Gladys just assumed he would do what he always did where she was concerned, nothing. Mrs. Wimble wore the pants in the family when it came to their daughter.

When Gladys walked into the sitting room of

their home and explained her goals, she braced herself for the backlash. What unfolded, however, was her mother starting in and her father shutting her up. He stood and walked to Gladys before giving her a suffocating squeeze and congratulating her on making her first adult decision on her own.

Gladys was floored. She assumed she would have a fight on her hands. Instead her mother sat in uncomfortable silence while her father helped her figure out how to accomplish it and making sure any bills to reach the goal would be paid.

Gladys knew her mother wouldn't and couldn't remain silent on this issue and eventually would say something. She didn't have to wait very long. It came later that night in the form of disappointment first. All the years she put into raising her right and she was just going to throw it all away.

Over time, the comments changed from sad and disappointed to angry and sarcastic. Her mother would say things like, "You will never find a decent husband now," or "You will be wiping snotty noses and scrubbing the floors your whole life, too, dear. If you wanted to befriend the help, I could have arranged that. You didn't need to become the help to achieve it."

Eventually, her mother accepted it. She didn't

like that she must, but she grew tired of fighting. Once Gladys obtained her certificate and had begun teach- ing, her mother gave up. She would still make comments, but they were back to the sad and disappointed kind. Her father beamed with pride. She went from being in the corner of her father's vision to the only thing he seemed to talk about.

Gladys was glad to move away. She loved her parents, but she didn't want to live her life like her mother. She realized the ones she didn't associate with were nicer than the ones she did. She always had to be something she wasn't with the chosen group. She could be herself with the others. Those school girls took a while to warm up to her. She didn't blame them. She would have been skeptical of the motives herself if the shoe were on the other foot.

Lesson learned. Now her goal was helping those students that passed through her door understand this as well. It didn't matter what you came from, it mattered who you chose to be.

She smiled as she looked over the young ones she was teaching. The children all had their heads bent and fingers busy working on their slates. She had given them several figures to work out on their own.

This age was eager to learn. They liked attending class.

She was adding more problems on the list when a noise from the back made her turn.

"Hello, Mr. Ulinski. What brings you by today?" Micha ducked in and approached the desk.

"I have what you asked for Miss, the words to "Bóg Się Rodzi." He held out the paper hoping she would just take it from him and he would be out of her way.

"Thank you." She turned to face the students, "Class? Please put your chalk down for a moment and look up here. This is Mr. Ulinski. He has been kind enough to write the words down to a song from Poland that he sings at Christmas time. Let's all give him a big thank you."

The class in almost unison said their thanks. "Mr. Ulinski. Would you mind singing it for us, so we can hear the rhythm of the song?"

He tugged a bit on his shirt collar. "Uh, well, sure, I guess. I'm not really a singer, though."

Gladys smiled and tried not to chuckle. "Not everyone has the voice of an angel, but I want the class to sing this right and they can't do that unless we know how it goes."

"Well, okay. Here, you can follow along with this.

I have it memorized." He passed her the paper and cleared his throat before beginning.

Gladys held the paper and read along as he sang. The song was about the birth of Jesus and the purpose of His physical birth. It was beautiful and powerful. As she followed, she realized he wasn't saying the words as they were exactly written. It was close, but a few were off. She attributed this to him knowing the Polish version and not the English translation.

Although, it did seem odd that if he wrote this, he should know what it said. She tucked that back and tried to pay attention. He had a lovely baritone voice for "not really being much of a singer."

When he finished, Gladys thanked him and the class chimed in after. As he was leaving, she noticed Miss Siller gawking from down the hall.

Gladys inwardly cringed as Miss Siller turned and walked back into her classroom. She knew how she and her friends would have spun this for their favor. What she didn't know was what to do regarding it. Should she wait it out to see if anything came of it or should she run to Mr. Davis and cut them off?

She turned back to the class and tried to move forward through the rest of her day. She had a difficult time staying focused, because her mind wandered back to what she saw when Mr. Ulinski left.

Gladys thought maybe she could explain to Miss Siller why he was there, but quickly dismissed it knowing it wouldn't change her mind on whatever she was set to do.

If she ran to Mr. Davis, he may be suspicious as to why a teacher observing concerned her.

She had yet to decide what to do by the time she dismissed the students. If she left it alone, it could end up spread all over town before she could try to rein it in.

Gladys was planning on cleaning Mr. Ulinski's home right after school today, but since he was home for the day already and they were seen together, she decided it would be best to avoid the area altogether for a while.

She walked back to the Kilpatrick's home, knowing this was one of her last times there. She would be moving over the weekend and that thought helped cheer her up a bit, but certainly left her nerves a bit unsettled.

She still hadn't been told where she was going. Then it dawned on her. She could wait until tomorrow before approaching Mr. Davis and seek him out to discuss her new living arrangements. If Miss Siller had brought up anything to him, he would most likely ask her about it then.

Hopefully enough time wouldn't have passed that the rumors spread beyond an easy clean up. Having a plan in place put a little bounce in her step and relaxed her regarding the situation. She wouldn't sleep easy tonight, but she would sleep better than she would have with no plan.

CHAPTER 18

*G*ladys awoke excited the next morning. That should have been her first clue that today would not go as planned. The Kilpatrick home had a way of draining all positive energy from her. The drab surroundings matched Mrs. Kilpatrick well.

Gladys wondered what the mistress of this home's life was like back in Ireland. She supposed it wasn't sunshine and rainbows if she wanted to leave it behind and come here to an unknown land.

Then again, she was married. It could have been her first husband's wish to move here for an opportunity for which Gladys didn't know. Moving here, two states away, was the first she had seen of anything outside her little life cocoon.

Despite her lack of friends, true friends, and her mother's overbearing authority over all her life, she did have a good childhood. She hadn't known true troubles. It made her wonder just how much of this world she really knew. Was her life common or were troubles more common? Did most suffer through? Or just some?

Shortly after Gladys awoke, Mrs. Kilpatrick approached her. She felt the need to remind Gladys that even though she was leaving today she was still here for a few hours and chores needed doing. She had added on a few that were not part of the normal routine, as well. She was most likely trying to get as much out of Gladys as possible before she was left to tend to it all by herself again.

While Gladys worked, she thought about what the next family might be like. Although she had an invitation to spend Christmas with the Crowley's, the bulk of the holiday time would be spent with this next family.

"What is Christmas like here?" Gladys asked Sarah as they scrubbed the wood floor.

Sarah paused mid scrub, head tilted up in thought. "Well, we don't work on Christmas, except for cooking. At night we exchange a few gifts.

Everyone gets one from someone else. We rotate each year who will make something for another. This year I have Papa. I'm knitting him a new pair of warm gloves in his favorite shade of blue. He loves the ocean blue and I tried to match it as close as I could. Momma helped me since I was too little when I was on the ocean and can't remember."

They returned to scrubbing in silence, Sarah unsure what else to say and Gladys thinking about the Kilpatrick Christmas.

"What is Christmas like in your home?" Sarah added to break the silence up.

Gladys smiled a little. "Christmas is a big affair and lasts for days. There are several of my parents' friends who host dinner parties and we rotate through them. The house is always decorated with evergreen boughs." Gladys looked at Sarah, who looked a bit sad, so she decided not to add in the abundance of presents she received.

Gladys felt a bit sad, too. This year Christmas would be very different for her. Then she mentally chastised herself. She was spoiled. She knew she was spoiled, but she was still learning just how much. "Your simpler Christmas sounds lovely... quiet and peaceful."

Sarah laughed. "It is not quiet. I have three brothers, but your Christmas sounds magical."

"Well, I wouldn't describe it that way. It's more chaotic and exhausting than magical." Gladys began scrubbing the floor with more enthusiasm. She thought she would spend the upcoming season missing home, but maybe here was where she needed to be.

It wasn't much longer when a knock sounded on the door. Sarah answered, and Mr. Davis stood asking if Gladys was ready to move. She was more than ready, but it appeared that Sarah was fighting back tears. Gladys gave her a hug as Mrs. Kilpatrick walked into the room.

"Mr. Davis, you are here earlier than I anticipated."

Mr. Davis gave a curt nod. "I hope that's not a problem. I would like Gladys to get to know the next family a bit before nightfall."

Mrs. Kilpatrick rubbed her hands together. "Yes, I suppose. Good bye, Gladys." She turned on her heel and walked back where she came.

Sarah shrugged her shoulders and Gladys shook her head. "My trunk is right there, sir," Gladys indicated by pointing her finger. "Let me take off this apron and clean up my hands, then I'll be ready."

Gladys took care of the few things she needed to and then hugged Sarah once more before closing the door on this strange, long month. It was pouring down rain outside and she didn't care. She was as light as if the sun was beating down on her face.

As they walked to his covered wagon Mr. Davis made small talk. "How is the cleaning going at Micha's, uh Mr. Ulinski's?"

"Well, I suppose. He seems happy with it."

He set the trunk down in the back and helped Gladys up the step and onto the bench. "Good. You are able to find time to do it when he is working, right?"

Gladys paused a moment.

Was he just checking in or had he heard something? "Yes, of course."

Mr. Davis settled in next to her and released the brake. "Good. Sounds like it's all working out all right then."

"Yes, sir."

They turned away from the main row of houses, most of them housing miners.

"You'll be staying at the Kemp home for this month. They live in a nicer and bigger place. I thought you might like that for the holidays."

Gladys was excited and wondered if this meant she might have a private sleeping arrangement.

"I do appreciate that, although, the families so far have been well enough." That didn't sound right, but the two homes were night and day. Saying wonderful would have described the Crowley's the correct way but wouldn't have represented her time with the Kilpatrick's.

Mr. Davis looked sideways at her. He apparently knew what she was thinking. "Mrs. Davis and I worked to set up the schedule before you came. Several families volunteered, and we arranged them in an order we felt was the best. We don't tell you ahead of time, though, since that order can change for a number of different reasons." Mr. Davis pulled the wagon over to the side of the road and set the brake. "If it wasn't raining so hard, we could have walked here."

Gladys took his hand as she climbed down. He fetched her trunk while she waited, looking at her surroundings. The two-story home stood taller than most.

That was promising for more space.

She kicked herself for thinking that.

Gladys gave an audible sigh and Mr. Davis

cocked his head with his brows drawn. "Relax. Come on. You will like them."

They walked up the front steps and onto the porch. Gladys took the opportunity while Mr. Davis knocked with his free hand to brush off the front of her dress. Her hair was limp and soggy from the little time out in the rain, but nothing could be helped for that.

"Hi, Charles," a jolly looking man said as he opened the door.

"Hey, a DJ."

The DJ fellow looked to Gladys and she gave a curt nod.

"DJ, this is Miss Wimble. Miss Wimble, this is Mr. Kemp."

"It's very nice to meet you, sir." Gladys tried to flash a relaxed smile, but she couldn't fight her nerves.

"Likewise." He stepped aside and welcomed them in.

"Oh, my. Come, here, stand by the fire and dry off a bit." A chestnut-haired woman spoke as she entered the room.

"Charles, follow me and I'll show you where to put that." Both men headed upstairs.

"Hi, I'm Mary. I see my wonderful husband failed to properly introduce us." She held her hand out with the back of her hand up in a delicate manner.

"It's so nice to meet you. I'm Gladys, but I'm sure you already knew that." Her cheeks grew rosy and warm.

"Yes, I do. I'm so glad you are here. We have been waiting our turn to host you. Can I get you anything? A cup of tea or coffee, or perhaps a towel?"

Gladys followed her eyes and realized her hair was dripping water onto the floor. "Oh dear, I'm so sorry ."

"Please stop. It can't be helped around here. We have hit the rainy season. Once we pull out of that it will be the snowy season, only to return once more to the rainy season." They chuckled.

"Would you rather I show you where you will be staying so you can freshen up a bit?"

Gladys closed her eyes and exhaled. "That would be lovely."

"Thank you for bringing her over. Mr. Davis. Please, excuse us gentlemen." They left the men talking work. "'Tis boring to listen to them once they get started on it."

"What does Mr. Kemp do?" Gladys already remembered that Mr. Davis was a pumpman.

"He is the mine foreman, complete with his very own office deep in the earth's belly."

"There's an office underground?" Gladys was truly shocked by this.

"There is, in fact. The mine is a big maze of different rooms and passageways. I've never been, of course, so if you want to know more details you will need to ask the miners themselves."

Gladys was thinking she should learn more. She had wanted to, but now she was intrigued she probably would seek it out instead of waiting for the information to come freely to her.

They stopped in front of a door that was two doors down from the top steps. "Here is your room, dear." She opened the door and Gladys was speechless. The room wasn't fancy, but it was a whole room with one bed just for her. She was feeling spoiled. A dresser stood below a window looking down to the street below and a soft plush rug lay where she would step when she climbed out of bed every morning.

"Oh, thank you. It is lovely!" Gladys wrapped her arms around Mary which caught her momentarily off guard.

"I'll leave you. When you are ready you can come down and find us. We can go over what daily life here is like and how to best fit your schedule in."

Mary closed the door as she left, and Gladys fell onto the bed like a little girl. She giggled a bit with her head in the pillow. This month was going to be a blessing.

CHAPTER 19

*A*nother work day dawned for Micha. He dressed in his grubby work clothes and rustled through the kitchen, hoping to find something for breakfast and lunch. He didn't have much but made himself a bowl of oatmeal and decided to swing into the company mess hall and buy a sack lunch for the day.

His money was precious. Living in the private home meant he shelled out more for housing. He tried to save where he could in other areas. Reducing what he ate and how much he ate was one of those.

Having Miss Wimble clean was a luxury he couldn't really afford, but he knew it was helping her and he wanted to do what he could. His house was

143

cleaner than before he'd moved in. Now it was just a matter of maintenance. She had been doing a fine job.

He patted Lady on the head and let her out for the day. She had a box he fastened together off to the side of the house for her to huddle in on days like today when the weather was cold and miserable. The rain was mixed with ice and Micha knew snow was approaching quickly. He crossed the street into the business district of town and entered the mess hall where many men were seated finishing their breakfasts.

"Hiya, Micha! Getting lonely over there by yourself? Ready to give up that darn dog of yours?" Jim hollered from a couple tables away.

"Mornin', Jim. Doing just fine, thanks for askin." Most liked to give him a hard time. He didn't take offense to the back and forth that would go on. Micha walked over to one of the ladies with lunches lined up on a table. "Morning, ma'am. I'd like whatever's on the menu for today, please."

She smiled sweetly at him, "Morning, Mr. Ulinski. We have egg salad sandwiches for today."

Not his favorite, but not the worst that could be served either. "Thank you much, ma'am."

He dropped his cents in her palm and snagged a

pail. A group of men started making their way up the trail, passing piles of logs that would be used to brace newly opened mining areas.

The head of the mine lay not far from town. The men walked uphill through a group of tall firs that led to an opening much smaller than town itself. It was the last of daylight they would see until their shift ended. The man cars would lower them into the belly of the earth.

The man cars ran on electricity. Three or four men would load into one of the two open metal boxes and ride it down to one of the three stops below. The first stop was eight hundred feet below, the second rested at twelve hundred feet, and the third took a man all the way to fifteen hundred feet below fresh air. The temperature remained even, regardless what the conditions were above ground; meaning in the winter time men would shed some clothing as they lowered. The mine ran twenty-four hours a day. Micha was fortunate he worked the day shift. About one hundred and fifty miners could be found working at any given time.

The tunnels had rail tracks running through them. As more coal was chipped away it could be loaded in metal boxes much like the ones that carried the men. The only difference between the boxes was the door that allowed the men to walk in and out. Also, the coal cars were tipped to remove the black rocks.

The piles of logs they passed when walking into work were found underground. They were used as beams running vertical up the walls and horizontal along the ceiling creating the look of separated rooms. In certain locations, miners would use them to crouch behind when the next blast was set to punch more tunnel and find more coal.

Micha found himself hunched on the lowest level of the mine, waiting for such a blast. With him were three other men, one was named Jakub. "I got another letter the other day. Will you help me read it?"

Jakub nodded. This wasn't the first time he'd helped Micha. They both hailed from different parts of Poland. Jakub could read, and he helped Micha stay in communication with his family. "Let me see. We have some time now."

Micha pulled the envelope from his pocket and pulled the letter out before handing it to Jakub. "Thanks again."

Micha always felt ashamed when he asked for help with reading, but Jakub never teased him. Some of the other men did. They thought it great sport to tease the big oaf with the dog that hated them all. Maybe because it was easy to redden his cheeks. He didn't know and really it didn't matter.

Jakub scanned the letter. "Says here they are still doing fine. They thank you for the money you send back and are putting it into the farm. Looks like your older brother and his wife have taken over most of the duties."

Micha was glad to hear that. His Tato was up in age and stubborn. All the kids wanted him to slow down, but he refused. Something must have made him slow down that Mamo wasn't mentioning, unless his Tato finally wised up.

"Fire in the hole!" They all covered their ears awaiting the explosion from the electric blasting cap that was attached to a stick of dynamite. As soon as the boom vibrated through the tunnel Jakob tossed Micha the letter and all three took off running to start shoveling the coal into the carts.

"Micha! Micha!" A deep voice was heard echoing down the tunnel.

Micha looked up from shoveling. "Ya?"

"Mr. Kemp's asking for you!" He shouted.

"Hey, thanks!" Micha shouted back. The other miners working with him started teasing him about having to see the boss. "Put a sock in it! I'll see what this is all about."

Mr. Kemp's office was on the third level, which made it a quick trip for Micha. His office was a cement box. The men all said he was scared of a cave- in or explosion and wanted the extra protection just in case. Micha knocked on his door.

"Enter."

Micha walked in and closed the door behind. The office was a cube that held no more than a desk and a couple of chairs. Mr. Kemp told him to sit.

"Hello, Micha. Tell me, how is the mine working today?" He sat with his hands folded on top of the desk and a small smirk on his face.

Micha shifted in the chair feeling oddly like he was in the hot seat despite the casual appearance of Mr. Kemp. "Everything on this level seems to be running smoothly. I'm not sure about the other two."

Mr. Kemp sat silently watching him for a moment. To Micha it felt much longer. "Do you enjoy your position?"

Micha was wondering if he was about to be fired. "I do, sir. It's honest, hard work. Can't complain."

"Good, good. Listen, I've been keeping tabs on you and I like what I see. You are a hard worker and you keep your nose clean. I'm thinking about moving you from laborer to apprentice for an electrician. What do you think about that?"

Micha's brows rose. "That would be great." An electrician made more which meant he could send more home.

"Good to hear it." Mr. Kemp stood, and Micha followed suit. He extended his hand and Micha pumped it, sealing the promotion. "You start tomorrow, first thing. Check in with Winchell. He'll be expecting you."

Micha left breathing easier despite all the dust that remained in his lungs. Being an electrician meant he would be working all over the mine instead of his current work that put him in the same place tunneling further in, day in and day out. He couldn't wait until he could sit down with Jakub and have him write all this down to send home. His parents would be mighty proud.

CHAPTER 20

Gladys had been staying with the Kemp's for a couple of weeks and she wasn't sure where the time had gone. Fortunately, Mary was nothing like Mrs. Kilpatrick. Gladys wasn't expected to do anything beyond picking up after herself and tending to her regular responsibilities at the school and at Mr. Ulinski's home. Those responsibilities were time-consuming.

Christmas was approaching rapidly, and Gladys found herself busier than ever. Since she'd rounded up volunteers to pull together the program, the other teachers pulled out of their portions completely.

Her intention in going door-to-door was to pull ideas for her portion of the program. She hadn't anticipated most wishing to help with the other areas. Gladys didn't want to say "no thank you" to an eager helper. She knew she would have upset the community if she did.

By encouraging and accepting their offers, she upset her coworkers. Gladys was caught and now she was realizing she had been left to pull off the whole event by herself. Miss Siller and Miss Dupont were upset with her. If Gladys was being honest with herself, she would have also been just as angry if she were in their shoes.

She loved working with the younger kids, but this was one of the times the older students would have come in handy.

She tried to encourage them. Gladys looked around at the children attempting to cut snowflakes. Some of them were decent, but many didn't remotely resemble a snowflake. The trick was in the fold, but not everyone got that down.

"Everyone, just keep trying. You'll get the hang of it soon."

She sighed and continued wandering around, helping where she could. She couldn't fail. That's what they were counting on. She was glad the class had started on the preparations early. Time was on her side and she would need everything she could get.

"Class, it's time to begin clean up. The end of our day is almost here." Several shouts of excitement were heard in addition to the continued sounds of frustration coming from the kids who were not pleased with their progress.

"We will have time to work on these again tomorrow. You can place your snowflakes on the tables by the window."

The children worked quickly in anticipation of being free for the rest of the day. Today was one of the rare non-rainy days, but it was cold.

Gladys let the children leave and stayed behind to finish cleaning up before she began her walk to the Kemp home. On her way out, she noticed a few papers sticking out from under a crate she was using to store the finished decorations. Upon further inspection, she realized they were her song sheets she had made for herself. That was just one more odd thing to happen since school started. She picked up the papers and tucked them into a drawer in her desk before finally leaving for the day.

She was mindlessly wandering when a doe stepped out into her path and froze. Gladys froze as well not sure what to do. The two stared at each other before the doe turned and entered the brush she had come from.

Gladys released a breath and thanked her stars it was just a deer that crossed her path. She had seen various animals and even deer before, although never this close. She didn't want to cross paths with a bear or cougar. Gladys quickened her pace and arrived at the Kemp's minutes later.

"Welcome home. Tea is hot on the stove if you'd like to warm up a bit."

Gladys shrugged off her coat. "Tea sounds lovely. It is quite chilly outside."

"Yes, I can feel snow. It's coming." Mary was working on needlepoint sitting in a rocker by the fireplace.

Gladys poured a cup of tea and joined her in the opposite chair. She held the cup with one hand resting it on the wooden arm of the rocker, and used her other hand to knead the back of her neck.

"Long day?"

She rolled her head a bit to stretch the muscles. "Yes, you could say that."

"I'm not sure how you do it. I would pull my hair out if I was responsible for that many children."

Gladys let out a quick, short breath as she

shrugged her shoulders. "They are great. It's the other adults in the building."

Mary looked up from her needlepoint with concern in her eyes.

Gladys supposed she couldn't redirect the conversation to another topic because now she felt like she was tattling or complaining. Her old self would have thought nothing of it. If someone was rude to her, she could say a few words to her mother or to her friends and the person would have been hit from so many different angles they wouldn't have known what to do.

She didn't want to revert back to her old self to take care of this problem. She also didn't have her group here to act. Gladys was alone.

Gladys told Mary the story of how she went in search of songs and ended up getting much more in return and how that affected the other classes.

Mary looked back down and continued threading her needle into the fabric stretched over the ring. "I see. They are upset and instead of talking to you they have dumped their work on you as a punishment."

"Oh, I don't think it's a punishment. I think they are just upset and think I have the whole thing done."

Mary chuckled. "It's a punishment dear. Miss Dupont and Miss Siller can be quite devious at times. I honestly don't know why they are still here teach- ing. Many of us do not like them, Mr. Davis seems oblivious. Not many want to teach here in the middle of nowhere so, I guess Mr. Davis doesn't have many options. He chooses to see what he wants"

Gladys wondered if they were truly the reason for the strange things that happened in her room.

Erasing the songs, having a dog interrupt, the missing broom, and having papers vanish were just a few of the oddities that had occurred. She wanted to hope that it was just silly pranks from students but knew it could have been the other teachers.

"Did others apply with me for this position?"

Mary nodded her head. "Yes, there was one other. It was a friend of Miss Dupont's. I think they really thought she would be hired. I'm glad Mr. Davis and the board chose you. You have been a wonderful addition to our community."

Gladys chewed on her lip, thinking about only two applying for a position that paid quite well. "Why don't people want to work here? It doesn't seem that bad and the pay is good, compared to other areas."

Mary set her needlepoint down on her lap. "The location isn't ideal. Not only are we a ways from areas that hold more excitement, but we get even more secluded at times in the winter months. You don't know it yet, but the snow gets deep and the trains have to stop regularly for the tracks to be cleared. Also, there is the mining issue. This life can be rough. I thank God that Mr. Kemp has a safer job. He's still under ground and I'm not too keen on that, but he sits at a desk and has the cement around him to help cushion any accidents. Unfortunately, accidents are common and frequent."

Gladys stared blankly at her with a feeling of unease washing over her. "What kind of accidents?"

"Oh, you really don't know dear? Explosions, cave ins, poisonous gasses."

Gladys' eyes grew large and her mouth fell open. Mary stopped talking abruptly.

"Those are just possibilities, Gladys. It doesn't mean that any of that will happen, although, deaths in mines are a regular occurrence everywhere. We've had a dry spell for a while and the whole town is grateful for that. We all know we are living on borrowed time, waiting for something to happen."

"What happens when *something* happens?" Gladys was gripping her teacup.

Mary picked her needlepoint back up and began to work

"Well, if we are lucky, it will just be one or two deaths. In that situation the body will be brought out. You might be one of the first to know of an accident, as the rescue equipment is stored in the storage rooms at the school." Mary glanced at Gladys, who was staring intently at her. "Normal funeral services and burial will be planned. Sometimes the family requests the body to be shipped back to where they came from. Other times they are put in the cemetery here. Then the family, if the man wasn't single, has two weeks. If they have a son that works in the mine, the mother and other children will be allowed to stay, but if not, they are gone. The house must be vacant for whoever will replace the lost miner."

Gladys had tears pooling in her eyes. "That's just so sad. It almost seems cruel."

Mary paused mid-poke of her needle. "Yes, it can be. It's business. The mine has to keep running."

"What happens if more than just one or two die?" Gladys didn't like this conversation, but she needed to know.

Mary looked over at Gladys, her eyes a bit glassy.

"Then we all go. If a major accident was to occur,

rendering the mine unable to run without significant cost to rebuild, the mine would shut down."

Gladys dropped her teacup and it shattered on
the floor, snapping both of their attention to the
mess of broken china and spilt tea. "Oh, I'm so
sorry."

"Nonsense. It was an accident. Let's clean it up
and talk about something lighter-hearted, please."
They both stood and began the cleanup in silence,
neither really knowing what to say next.

CHAPTER 21

icha's official new title was electrician's helper. He hoped he could hold on to that and eventually move up, but learning the ropes proved more difficult than he'd anticipated.

He hadn't realized how much reading was involved. Different portions of the mine were controlled by breakers. If a piece of equipment wasn't working properly, he had to figure out which breaker needed flipped before they could work on it. If he could read the labels attached to each one, that portion of the job would be simple. Instead, he was working hard to memorize them and hoping no one would figure out he was illiterate in the process.

Micha was tired and frustrated and decided an evening with the guys wouldn't break the bank, especially now that his new position meant a raise in pay.

Georgetown, which was adjacent to Ravensdale, held close to a dozen saloons. There was also a selection of dance halls to pick from, but Micha was not a dancer, nor did he care to mingle with the fairer sex.

Micha glanced up and down the street and decided The Royal George would suit his needs fine. He wasn't much of a drinker, and never cared for the way it made him feel when he over indulged. Sipping on one or two while he caught up with the guys would be plenty.

Micha stepped over the threshold and shucked his coat, hanging it on an empty peg. He found a seat at the bar and sat down. A middle-aged balding man wearing a white apron took his order. As the vodka was set in front of him, Micha was slapped on the shoulder and Jakub took a seat to his right.

"Well, well, well. It seems the recluse has decided to grace us with his presence."

Micha took a sip and rolled the tepid liquid over his tongue a bit before swallowing. "Hey, Jakub."

"Micha." Jakub was curious as to what made him

all the sudden show up in a place like this. "How's the new job going?"

Micha sighed. "It's going. A bit of a learning curve it has, but I'll get the hang of it."

Jakub nodded in agreement. "I can imagine. Glad you got the opportunity."

"Thanks!"

"What do we have here?"

Micha didn't have to turn and look to see who was behind him. Luka was someone he usually avoided. Fortunately, he worked on a different level and they rarely crossed paths.

"Hiya, Luka." Micha raised his shot glass and took another sip.

Luka grinned. "Drink it like a man, Micha. Sipping vodka!" A belly laugh began low and rolled its way up and out of the stout fellow. He waved his hand in dismissal and stepped away to find his own seat.

Luka's presence made Micha remember why he hated coming to these establishments. He began to stand to leave when Jakub put his hand on his shoulder.

"Don't let him get under your skin."

Micha looked over at Jakub and raised a brow while shrugging. He sat back down and took another sip making his shot about half gone. Jakub raised his hand to the bartender for another round for Micha.

"Oh no, one's plenty."

"It's on me. I don't see you around much since you moved out. I'd like to catch up. I don't know why I come here. It's the same men I live with. No good, many of them. They work just to party here."

Micha snorted. "And that is why I chose Lady over all those lovely fellows."

They both looked over as a group of half a dozen men were beginning to get a bit rowdy. The night would be lively here. Micha wouldn't stay long enough to see it.

"Hey, Micha!"

Both Jakub and Micha turned their heads to see who was hollering. It appeared another trouble-maker was jumping in where Luka left off.

"Why you here tonight? That little lady teacher reject you?"

Micha was confused. "You mean Miss Wimble?"

The group started laughing. "Yeah, that's the one. Hear she's been coming over...regularly."

"Ignore them, Micha." Jakub tried to pull him back.

"Listen, I don't know what you are talking about. Miss Wimble cleans my house when I'm at work.

She is a very nice, proper lady, so you best stop talking about her."

An "oh" could be heard amongst several of them.

"Why so defensive, Micha? Did we hit a nerve?"

"Micha!" Jakub warned him.

Micha stood and faced the man. Jakub stood next to him.

"You better shut up. She is a good lady and deserves respect."

"Hey fellas, it seems Micha might be fallin' for the teacher," Luka chimed in.

Micha made a move forward, but Jakub grabbed him and pulled him to the door, calling behind him to put the drinks on his tab.

"Come on. We don't need this."

The two walked to Micha's in the dark. Lady met the pair at the road.

"Why don't we write back home and tell them about the promotion?" Jakub encouraged.

Micha agreed that would be better time spent then tending a sore fist from defending Miss Wimble's character, although he wasn't entirely sure why the need grew so strong. She had her rough edges and they certainly didn't start off on the right foot. Over time, though, he saw her true self.

Micha fed Lady then found a piece of paper for

Jakub to write on. He began dictating what Jakub would write. After a few short minutes Jakub was reading back to him the letter explaining his new position, letting them all know he was well, and inquiring about them.

"You made the job seem easy in the letter. What had you upset about it earlier?"

Micha hated questions like this. Talking about his lack of intelligence was not something he enjoyed. "The job is not just wait for the blast, pick at the coal, load it in the carts, and repeat. There is a lot to it. If I could read it would help."

"What do you need to read?" Jakub was confused. As far as he knew, electrical meant wires not words.

"Each of the breakers that control the power supply are labeled. Without hesitation, I need to know which breaker belongs to what. If there is an emergency, I can't take my time trying to figure it out or hoping I guessed right. I need to know."

Jakub squinted and looked up at the ceiling. "I see." He tapped a finger on the table. "Maybe there is a way I can help you memorize them."

Micha was willing to do whatever. He wanted to keep this job.

"Let me look around. We need to get our hands on a diagram so we can begin working."

Micha pumped Jakub's hand and gave his back a pat. "Thank you! Thanks for all your help."

"Eh, don't mention it. I'm going to head on out. I'll let you know if I figure something out."

The guys parted, and Micha, for the first time that day, was feeling hopeful.

CHAPTER 22

*R*eady or not, the Christmas program was about to begin. The community had already begun filling the gym. Sylvia and Mary were directing traffic and handling the food and beverages. Mr. Kemp and Mr. Crowley had set up a tree in the corner. The children hung paper chains and ribbon scraps their mothers had donated for the occasion prior to the doors being opened for the town. Gladys had hung some sheets with the help from both the Crowley's and the Kemp's. If it wasn't for those families she didn't know what she would have done. The children were all hiding behind the sheets, waiting for their cue to begin singing.

Her portion of speaking was quick. She had a speech written down, but it seemed to have grown legs and walked away. She wasn't too concerned, though, as a little thank you for coming and an "I hope you enjoy" was all that was needed.

The kids moved through the part in the sheets and lined up in practiced rows. They knew what to do. Gladys stood off on the side and watched, ready to step in and get them back on track, if needed. She had them start with one that many of them already knew, saving the new foreign ones for later when they had time to calm their nerves a bit first.

Gladys used this time to scan the crowd. Many of these people she had yet to meet, despite living here for several months already. Some of them she had been introduced to, but only a few could she call friends. Not counting any of the children, there were only two and those two were the only souls willing to give her a hand.

The children were silent after finishing the previous song. It seemed they all forgot which one was next. Gladys gave them their cue to start "O Tannenbaum." They started a bit shaky but recovered quickly .

Gladys began paying more attention to the audience as this was the start of their portion mixing different cultures. Many people were confused, except a few that were lip synching along, which grew into full voices joining the children.

With each song, different people would join in, singing in their native tongue. Gladys fought to keep her composure. What she hoped would happen was happening, and everyone seemed very happy.

Miss Siller and Miss Dupont glared at Gladys with each passing song. Gladys was doing no harm, only trying to bring some joy to everyone. They, of course, wouldn't see it that way. Everything Gladys did would be wrong.

With the final songs concluding, it was time to mingle and eat. Gladys was apprehensive about this portion of the evening the most. She watched her class as they finished the last line of "We Wish You A Merry Christmas," and the audience clapped and cheered. She looked over her pupils, feeling proud of what they'd accomplished.

Sylvia took her place behind the refreshments tables and Mrs. Kemp was in a conversation with a few older ladies. Gladys made sure all the kids made their way back to their parents before stationing herself by Mrs. Crowley.

"That was wonderful, dear."

Gladys beamed. "You really think so? I was very nervous it wouldn't go over as hoped."

"Nonsense." Sylvia was assisting the first few making their way through the refreshments.

As people moved through, some of them thanked Gladys for the evening, many smiled at her, a few ignored her completely. She tried not to read into those too much. Gladys had yet to meet many of the townsfolk given that she really wasn't allowed out and about outside of school. She chalked up the ignoring to just not being introduced yet.

Gladys kept scanning the room, making sure everyone was having a good time. Miss Siller and Miss Dupont seemed to split up and were mingling with the community separately.

"Why don't you go wander around?" Mrs. Crowley said as she continued helping people.

Gladys' eyes showed panic. "Oh no, I couldn't. I barely know anyone here."

"Well, you can stay here with me if you like. I would introduce you, but I'm a bit busy." Sylvia began waving someone to come over.

"Micha, why don't you escort Miss Wimble around and introduce her to the town?" Sylvia smiled and encouraged.

What was Sylvia up to?

Micha looked at Gladys who ducked her head. "I'd be glad to. Miss Wimble, this way."

Gladys pinched her lips and cocked them to the side while she glanced at Sylvia who just smirked back. She planted a pleasant smile on her face and tucked her arm into Micha's bent one. Together they began circling the room.

Gladys would never remember all the names she would be hearing, but this was the first real step in making herself a permanent fixture in the community and not just the school.

As they made the rounds, she slowly started to realize that some people seemed to deliberately be moving away from them and others she caught staring at her, including Miss Dupont and Miss Siller.

Gladys chastised herself mentally, saying those that moved away were nervous to meet her and the stares were just plain curiosity. It wasn't until she realized those that were behaving this way were people who had spoken with one of the other teachers prior, that she began to start questioning her thinking.

Mr. Davis began staring at her which made Gladys nervous. Gladys looked up at Micha who was wrapped in pleasant conversation with the current folks he had introduced her to, and she was standing next to him with her arm still looped through his as a couple would.

Gladys removed her arm and looked up to Micha. "Oh dear, I'm sorry but I must head back over to Sylvia, Mrs. Crowley." She turned to those folks in front of her. "It was a pleasure meeting you. Micha, thank you for introducing me." Gladys walked briskly back and took her place next to Sylvia once again.

"You're back soon," Sylvia said in between doling out spoonsful of some type of pudding.

"Yes. I couldn't leave you here working too long without me." Gladys chewed the inside of her cheek.

"Oh, there is more to it than that. Spill it!"

Gladys sighed. "Mr. Davis spotted us and, based on his look, I assumed he thought we were being a bit too friendly with each other."

"I'm not sure why he would think that. You two were behaving in proper fashion."

"I hope so. I really love teaching and don't want to jeopardize my place here. My heart is in education and I don't know what I'd do if I couldn't do that."

The evening finished with Gladys, the Kemp's, the Crowley's, and the other two teachers cleaning up. They tried to dodge out, but Mr. Crowley spotted them and reined them back in.

Gladys figured this was their plan all along. They chose not to help with any of the set up and they would skip out on the cleanup as a punishment for Gladys overstepping her bounds. Gladys was beginning to think she would never form any kind of relationship with them.

All in all, the night was a success despite the warning look she got from Mr. Davis and the random stares that came from complete strangers. Gladys wasn't sure she would ever know what that was about, and she wasn't so sure she wanted to.

CHAPTER 23

Gladys found herself sitting in the middle of the room Christmas morning with the Kemp's. It felt off. The calendar said Christmas, but aside from some decorations, it felt like a normal day. Mary tried. She fixed a grand breakfast, and instead of that filling her with cheer, she just felt bloated and cramped. They were sipping on coffee and Gladys was trying to keep down what she had eaten. It all wanted to come back up to relieve the pressure from overeating.

They were having a conversation of pleasantries and Gladys was mostly just listening. It wasn't until she heard Micha's name that she focused in more on what Mr. Kemp was saying.

"He seems to be doing much better now. I'm not

sure the change, but in the beginning, he was struggling to keep up. He's always been a hard worker and quick to learn, but with this job I thought for sure I'd have to demote him."

"Well then, I'm glad things turned out." Mary took another sip of her coffee before taking Mr. Kemp's and hers to get a refill. She asked Gladys if she would like more as well.

"Oh, no thank you Mary. I think I've had all I can handle for the moment." She set the cup on the table next to her. "Everything this morning was very delicious, though. Thank you."

Before Mary left to go fill just the two cups, she paused in front of Gladys. "I'm very sorry that you can't be with family this year. I do know what that feels like. Of course, I have Mr. Kemp here to help ease the loss I feel for not being with the rest. You don't even have anything to open this morning. I wish I would have thought of something you needed. I just kept drawing a blank, though, as you don't have a permanent residence to keep much."

Gladys waved her hand. "I will be just fine with what I have but thank you for thinking of me."

Mary left for the kitchen and Gladys turned her attention to Mr. Kemp. "So, Micha is doing well with learning the electrical portion of the mine?"

"Oh, yes. It was the strangest thing. He stumbled for weeks and then it was just like a switch was thrown and power connected in his brain. Much like it works in the mine, you see. We have breakers that flip power on and off to various portions of the mine and equipment. Micha struggled to learn the routing despite having sufficient labels on every one."

Gladys mulled that information around. She assumed, based on the past information she had learned, that it was his lack of reading skills that was the culprit.

How he quickly made up for that disadvantage was the puzzle. If she could figure that out maybe she could help future students who struggled with reading. "Well, I'm happy everything has worked out." She didn't want to tip off his boss on her questioning of his skills.

Mr. Kemp opened his mouth to speak as Mary entered with fresh coffee. "Here we are."

"Thank you, dear." He took his cup and must have decided on not continuing with his thought. Mary took control of the conversation and directed it to spring and baseball.

Just as her stomach was calming and feeling relaxed, midday approached and with that came time to switch houses for the day. Gladys was to spend Christmas evening with the Crowley's. She hoped she could find more Christmas cheer there for Sadie andJeffrey, if not for herself.

Mr. Kemp donned his thick coat and hat and waited for Gladys to do the same. The weather held a bite and snow had been on the ground for a few weeks. While it looked beautiful, it made for treacherous walking. The temperature didn't rise above freezing during the day, causing the top layers of snow to turn to solid ice. Slipping was a hazard she wouldn't have to face today with Mr. Kemp driving her over.

When Sadie saw Gladys, she threw open the door and locked her arms around Gladys's waist. "Merry Christmas Gladys!"

Gladys wished a merry Christmas back to Sadie as she gently pried the little girl off her long enough to enter the small, but cozy house.

The warmth from the fire immediately began seeping into her bones and the smells of cinnamon, nutmeg, and ginger brought a feeling of home that worked to relax her shoulders and ease her melancholies from earlier.

They had a small tree in the corner that was held by a wooden cross at its base. Popcorn had been strung around the branches and under the tree held a few packages wrapped in plaid fabrics. A larger crate was placed along the wall next to the tree and Gladys wondered what was in it, but didn't outright ask.

Sylvia walked in from the bedroom carrying another bundle wrapped in plaid and set it under the tree. "Oh, you're here! We can start."

"You waited for me?" Gladys was a bit surprised by that.

Sadie began jumping up and down, "Yes, yes! Momma said we couldn't open gifts or eat any treats until you got here. And now you're here so let's start, please." She turned to her mother with pleading eyes.

"Oh, Sadie!" Sylvia shook her head and chuckled. "Let Gladys get in and settled first."

"You all waited for me?" Gladys looked around the room as a feeling of love washed over her. Jeffrey was sitting at the table, his game abandoned, looking at her with excited eyes.

"Of course, dear." Sylvia walked to Gladys and took her coat. "Children, please go get Gladys a cup of cider."

The kids rushed off as Gladys was sitting down in a chair by the fire. They came back carrying a steaming mug of cider and a cookie. "Momma, can we have a cookie, too?" Sadie turned her doe eyes to her mother.

"You may each have one. I don't want you spoiling your dinner." Sylvia turned back to Gladys and took the chair next to her as the children both ran off to pick their treat. "James spent all day yesterday out hunting. He brought home a nice fat goose for me to cook today."

Gladys looked around the room. Not only was the tree decorated, but garland had been hung over the door, on the mantel, and in the middle of the table with red candles placed atop. The whole cozy area was beautiful, and the smell of evergreen mixed with roasting bird along with the simmering cider and burning candles smelled of Christmas.

"What does everyone do for Christmas around here?"

Sylvia took a sip of cider before answering. "Well, I'm sure most have their own traditions and are partaking in whatever those are now. We keep to ourselves on Christmas Day. I'm sure most do, as the town remains fairly quiet. All but the single men's quarters, that is."

Gladys hadn't thought of the residents without families. "They must feel very homesick this time of year."

"I'm sure they do, although they are together. I've helped before on the meal, so I can say they eat well. Many of them hunt the few days before and a group of us ladies prepare a big feast for them. They usually don't have decorations and I don't think they exchange gifts, but I know they save letters from home from the previous weeks and take turns reading them out loud."

"That sounds sad though."

Both women sipped their cider and sat silent for a moment. "It does indeed," Sylvia stated.

Mr. Crowley came through the door and removed his hat and coat before stepping to the fire. "Sure is a cold one. Looks like more snow might be on its way, too."

The kids both squealed in excitement for snow. Sylvia got up and gave Mr. Crowley a warm mug of cider. "I think we should do presents before these kids start bouncing off the walls in excitement."

The kids started jumping up and down which made the adults in the room laugh. "All right children, go pick out something to open." James settled into a third chair to watch.

Jeffrey's gift contained a slingshot and he immediately began pretending to fire at some far-off beasts in his imagination. Sadie opened up a package with new handmade doll furniture for her doll house. She hugged them to her chest. Mr. Crowley got up and passed a gift to Sylvia. It contained a lovely hair clip with green gems fixed to a golden scroll design.

"Oh, it's lovely." Sylvia stood and walked into their room. She came out with the clip placed neatly in her hair. She bent down and kissed her husband's cheek while he took his hand in hers.

Gladys looked on at the touching moment. Her parents never behaved in such a way in front of anyone, including her. She wasn't entirely sure they behaved that way in private, either. She was lost in thought until Mr. Crowley began pushing the large crate towards her, making a scraping sound on the floor. It stopped directly at her feet. Gladys was confused.

"Well, open it up," Sylvia looked on in anticipation. "James can start it with the prybar."

Mr. Crowley loosened the top of the crate and stood back so Gladys could fully open it. She stood to lift the lid off and set it aside. Everything was covered in straw. When she moved the straw aside, she found a letter on top. She set that in her vacated chair before continuing to dig through.

Inside she found her things - the items she

decided not to bring with her from home. The same items she was glad weren't currently here due to lack of space to keep them. Under the supplies of kitchen items and bedding were wrapped garments. She pulled those out and opened them.

Sylvia gasped, "Those are lovely dear."

Tears formed to Gladys' eyes. "But I don't understand."

The Crowley's looked at each other with concern. "Read the note. Maybe the answer's in there."

She placed the dress back into the crate and turned to pick up the letter. Carefully opening it, she saw her mother's script.

MY DEAREST GLADYS,

Merry Christmas, darling. I hope this finds you well. Your father and I are very sorry we couldn't be with you this holiday season. It is our first apart and I'm afraid my heart does break from it. I know you were not exactly expecting these items as last we heard you were still living with various people just like a common boarder. Tsk tsk dear. I don't know how you can live like that. I've sent your belongings along with a few new dresses in the hopes it will push you to find a more permanent solution to your housing. The dresses will only help turn the heads of the men. Please consider only those of a certain class. Only the ones who could afford to buy you similar dresses would be approved by your father and me. I know you will look so lovely in them and that every man will give his best try. I'm just sorry I cannot be there to witness the commotion your prettiness will cause.

Lovingly yours,

Mother

Gladys let the letter fall back to her chair as she dabbed her eyes with her sleeve, very unladylike, but she didn't care.

Sylvia stood and placed her hand on Gladys' back. "What's wrong dear?"

Gladys hiccupped. "Everything. Just everything." She turned to look out the window. "I'm sorry I'm spoiling your Christmas."

"Nonsense. Come back and sit. Talk to us, please."

Gladys did that, although she would have rather fled out the door. "This." She waved her hand over the crate. "Everything in here I left behind. I was going to send for them when I had someplace to keep it all. Now, I'll have to lug it from house to house and hope it's not in anyone's way."

Mr. Crowley steepled his hands. "You can leave the crate here with us. We'll keep it for you until you have a permanent residence."

"Yes, of course," Sylvia added. "I'm sure you can put those beautiful dresses to use now, though."

"No, I can't." Gladys shook her head. "As a teacher I'm required to wear plain dark dresses. Mother knows this. She did this to encourage me to find a husband. It's all in the letter. If I step out in any of those I'll be reprimanded, if not fired, for breaking a contract that I signed."

"I see. Well, those can stay here in the crate as well then."

Gladys did not want to impose upon this family any more than she already felt she had. "I know. Sylvia, why don't you enjoy my dresses. We are close to the same size. I'm sure with minimal alterations they would fit."

Sylvia looked between Gladys and James. "Oh no dear. I couldn't."

"Yes, I insist. It will be my present to you."

"While the thought is greatly appreciated, I won't be fitting into my current clothes in a short time."

Sylvia looked at James. "Merry Christmas. My present to you this year is another bundle."

Gladys' crate and contents were all but forgotten by all but Gladys in that moment. The Crowley family's excitement for a new baby took over. Gladys was excited for them as well, but her mother had, like in most happy occurrences in the past, put a damper on the day.

The children continued with opening a couple more gifts and it seemed the crate issue was behind everyone but her. Gladys knew they would keep the crate. She just hoped it wouldn't become a burden to them. She wanted a permanent housing solution, but currently that goal was only a dream.

"We do have one more gift. If you all would wait a moment I'll bring it out." Mr. Crowley went into the bedroom and came out carrying a wooden chair.

"I helped Papa make the chair," Jeffrey offered. And Momma and I sewed the cushion," Sadie all but shouted. The children were both excited.

Mr. Crowley set the chair down in front of Gladys. "Me? This is for me?"

"Of course, dear. A new chair for your classroom. This one should be more comfortable than the one you currently have." Sylvia smiled at Gladys.

Gladys stood from her current chair to sit in the

new one. She took her hands and rubbed her palms over the smooth armrests. The pad was very thick under her and the colors of the fabric, a floral pattern of reds and oranges, brought a smile to her face and a warmness in her heart.

These people she had just met a few short months earlier knew her and what she would want better than her own mother. She didn't know how that was possible. "Thank you all so very much. I love it."

Hugs were exchanged before the goose was pulled from the oven. Everyone sat at the table to dig into the delicious smells that made all their stomachs rumble in anticipation.

Gladys watched them all with adoration. These people were quickly becoming a big, important part of her life. With the crate, and the emotions it brought, completely behind all of them now, they continued on with their Christmas celebration. Games would follow dinner and Gladys was warmed by love from all.

CHAPTER 24

*W*inter had dug its feet in and wasn't letting up anytime soon. The temperatures were freezing, and a heavy coat no longer provided enough insulation to keep the chill away. Trying to walk in the feet-deep snow in a dress was near impossible, but Gladys had no other choice. The other teachers didn't have the walk that she did, and the dress code didn't allow for her to dress for the inclement weather. By the time she would reach school each morning her dress would be soaked wet to her knees and her lower legs frozen and numb. With Christmas long past and weeks yet of bitter cold and hard walks ahead for everyone, she knew the kids could use some cheer. Gladys had brought some of her seeds with her tucked safely into a pocket within the folds at the top of her skirt.

She had selected Bachelor Buttons, Sweet Williams, and Snapdragons. The children could choose which they wanted for their homes. They would not plant them today, but she could tell the children of her plans and let them know they would need to bring in something to plant them in, as well as soil.

The men would need to help with that since the ground was frozen solid and she didn't think even the oldest boys in her class would be able to break through enough ground to get good quality soil for their containers.

Once the flowers were planted, she could teach them about germination, parts of a plant, and how to care for them. They would have specimens to observe as they learned.

Arriving at school, her first chore was to start the fire. Everyone would appreciate the warm room and source of heat to stand by to dry off. Given the abundance of coal, her stove that was installed in the new building was made for that type of fire.

Coal was messy to handle, but Gladys had gloves for just that purpose. The coal dirt would stay on the outside and her hands inside would remain clean. It burned dirty as well, and Gladys had begun cleaning coal dust from the surfaces in the school room like she did at Micha's home.

Gladys turned when she heard a noise at the door, expecting to greet her first children. Instead she saw Micha holding his hat in hand.

"Sorry if I startled you." He stepped across the threshold, but stood close to the door.

Gladys took her hand to smooth her tied up hair, "No, you didn't. I thought I had some early students is all. Please come in. The fire is just getting going, but it will be warm shortly. You could stand next to it if you'd like."

"No sense in warming up. I'm on my way up the hill to work. I saw you trudging through the snow, though, and wanted to ask if you needed some help to and from each day. Just while the snow lasts, of course."

Gladys warmed with love. She hadn't found many friends here, but the ones she had were wonderful. "I'm hoping the snow doesn't last much longer, but I can manage until then. I do appreciate the offer."

Micha paused a moment with his lips pinched together. "I could talk to Mr. Davis and see if he had an idea to help you. It really is no trouble. Besides, the snow here could last several weeks yet. Once winter hits it likes to stay sometimes until May."

Gladys certainly hoped it wouldn't last until May. That would be several more months yet to deal with it. Realizing now that Micha didn't mean himself helping her directly made his offer a bit easier to accept. Gladys had to be very careful. Just standing here alone with this single man could cause tongues to wag and her job on the line. "I don't want to cause undue trouble for anyone, but I would appreciate thinking about a possible way to get me here and home easier. It's so cold and it takes half the day to completely thaw."

Micha smiled. "I'll see what I can do. I should get going so I'm not late to work." He placed his hat back atop his head and then added, "I left your pay on the table this morning. I do appreciate all your help and I'm glad there is something more I can do to try and help you."

He left Gladys smiling. Between him and the Crowley's she was starting to feel somewhat at home. Gladys would like to have more people she could call friends, or at the very least acquaintances, but it was a start. The sound of little voices reminded her that she had many more who were friendly to her than just those few adults. The children warmed her heart and she treasured her time with each of them.

MICHA PULLED himself up the hill through the knee- high snow, thankful that the holiday season was over. He'd take a mountain of snow over being lonely for home when being with family was the foremost in everyone's mind. The guys' Christmas was all right, he supposed. Of course, the food was great. Sitting around a big room telling jokes back and forth and playing cards didn't replace his mamo and tato. He hoped he would be together with them again one day .

One good thing about where he worked was that regardless of what it was like outside, underground the temperature stayed the same. He wouldn't have to deal with the snow until he made his way home at day's end. His first order of business was to seek out Mr. Davis and express his concern.

Finding Mr. Davis wasn't hard. Trying to figure out how to broach the subject was another story. Micha hoped Mr. Davis wouldn't read too much into his concern. While he did think Gladys was a terrific catch, he didn't want others knowing he felt that way. Micha wasn't sure himself exactly how he felt about her. As he got to know her a bit better, he realized there was much more to Gladys Wimble than the woman he first saw.

"Charles!" Micha shouted to Mr. Davis to get his attention. He was ahead of him ready to enter the man car to take him down to work. "Hold up a minute."

Mr. Davis stopped and waited for Micha to reach him. "Morning Micha. How ya doing?"

Micha tucked his hands into his pockets to hide his nervousness and warm them up a bit. Why he was so nervous he didn't quite understand. "I'm good. Cold, but that's to be expected this time of year. How are you?"

"Doing well, but I, too, am cold and anxious to get to work so I can warm up."

Micha nodded. "Of course. Right. So, I was wondering if there was something to be done to help Gla, uh, Miss Wimble, sir? She has to walk in this snow, too, and, well, being in a dress and all it doesn't make it real easy. I thought maybe we could find a solution to help her out."

Mr. Davis pinched his lips to try to hide his chuckle from Micha. "Do you have a suggestion?"

Micha danced between his feet. "Well, no. I just know she has a problem. I'm not sure how to fix it."

"Son, I do appreciate you helping to look after our newest teacher, but this is the job she signed on for. If she has a problem with it I'm sure she will come to me."

Micha pulled a hand free from his pocket and rubbed the back of his neck. "Yes, sir. Of course." He abruptly turned and headed for work, leaving Mr. Davis standing with his arms folded across his chest and a big smile on his face.

Micha wasn't sure what to do to help Gladys, but he knew he really wanted to. She didn't have many people here to look out for her. Maybe that was the reason he cared so much.

Micha was falling for her, but perhaps it was just because she was like his Lady. He was always attracted to females needing help. He knew there was something he could do to help her, however small it may be. There was always something that could be done in any situation.

He didn't have a buggy or an automobile, so giving her a lift was out of the question. Not to mention, he was a single man and that was forbidden. Giving her different clothes that would make the walk easier would breach the contract she signed as well.

Micha understood the need for rules in any profession. It kept things orderly, but sometimes those rules were a bit asinine. Sometimes rules needed to be bent at times. Then the idea struck him. If he left for work a little early, he would have time to stop at the school to start the fire. She would still have to walk and would still end up wet from the knees down, but the room would be warm, and she could start to dry off sooner.

All he would need is Mr. Davis to loan him a key. With a solid plan to help ease Gladys' struggles, Micha set to work with renewed vigor. He always felt great when he was able to help someone else. It wasn't exactly how he was hoping to help her, but it would help nonetheless.

CHAPTER 25

*G*ladys was getting used to her classroom being warmed before she arrived. She had yet to confirm her suspicions of Micha being behind this lovely warmth. The conversation about helping her out a few weeks ago added to her beliefs. She wouldn't out right ask him. It was better she didn't know anyway. No rumors could be twisted, saying she was worming her way into Micha's life.

The last time Micha stood in this room with Gladys was the same day she presented her seed idea to the children. They loved it. Well, most of them anyway. Some of the boys couldn't have cared less if they planted flowers or not. Containers of all sorts had been trickling in for the seeds.

Today she would be receiving the soil. Mr. Crowley had filled a wheelbarrow after he first scraped away the snow and then picked through the frozen layers to get to workable material. She appreciated it greatly and wasn't sure how to repay him for the hard work.

Gladys instructed the children to retrieve their containers. They would be heading outside to fill them with soil before tucking the seeds in. She remained by the windows, watching for Mr. Crowley who would be there at any moment.

The containers ranged from wood to metal to glass. A few children had brought glass jars with very narrow openings in them. They had to return those and find something easier - to not only put seeds in, but to remove the plants once they were ready to be planted outside. She knew that was the hardest part of this whole endeavor.

Gladys hoped she wouldn't need to break any containers to get the flowers out and with enough dirt still surrounding their roots to limit shock when transplanting.

Just as the last child was sitting down, she spotted Mr. Crowley. Gladys instructed the children to make a single-file line so she could lead them outdoors. She had never led them out the front.

Normally, the only outside time would be spent on the playground. She liked the outdoors, when it was warm, and hoped to get the class outside more often soon.

"Good morning, Mr. Crowley." The class joined in wishing him a good morning. Sadie ran up and jumped into his arms.

Mr. Crowley kissed his daughter on her forehead before setting her back down. "Good morning, Miss Wimble, class. I hope I have enough dirt here for you. 'Twas difficult digging, but I'm happy to be of help."

"And we are all very happy you provided this for us."

Mr. Crowley dusted his hands on the legs of his pants. "If you don't mind, I can leave this right here for you and come back for it after work today. I did get a pass for a little while, but I should get going."

"Of course! Thank you again." Gladys turned to her students and gave them an encouraging look to thank Mr. Crowley themselves, which they did.

Mr. Crowley left after giving Sadie one more hug and Jeffrey a ruffle of his hair. Gladys instructed the children to form two lines, one on either side of the wheelbarrow so they could fill their own containers.

Doing it two at a time would save time. Most of

the children worked quickly to fill their containers. She had a few that tried to play in the dirt and Gladys stepped in and helped them finish. As she lined the kids up to head into the classroom, she told them they would be planting their seeds later in the day. Gladys wanted the soil to warm first before the seeds touched it.

She held the door open to let the students enter and Miss Siller greeted her. "Well, I see you must have had a visitor. What are these children doing outside right now?"

Gladys was taken aback. She didn't think she broke any rules by leading the kids out front. "I'm sorry if something is amiss. Mr. Crowley brought us some soil so we can plant our flower seeds and move ahead with our botany lessons."

Miss Siller looked at all the children. "Mr. Crowley, was it? I thought maybe it was Mr. Ulinski. He seems to come daily for you now. Be careful Miss Wimble, I would hate to see Mr. Davis let you go for breach of contract." Miss Siller turned on her heel and headed back to her room.

Gladys stood open-mouthed before pulling herself together to escort her class back to their room. She wasn't sure what to do about Micha now. She loved the warm room each day but wouldn't allow that to come between her and this job. Gladys loved the children and this was one of the only positive things she had here.

Talking to Mr. Davis was the most likely approach to head off any potential threat with this. And that was exactly where she was headed right after school. She would be getting moving orders any day now as well. Maybe she would save him a trip to her this way .

Mrs. Davis met her at the door. She had a sack and must have just come from the company store. Gladys hadn't much need for the store since she stayed with others. That allowed her to save her money in the hope that by school years end she would have enough to get her own place.

"I'll take that for you."

Mrs. Davis passed off the bag and thanked Gladys. She held open the door for Gladys to pass through and directed the bag to be placed on the counter for later. "I haven't seen you in a while dear. Let me set the coffee on and we can catch up a bit."

Gladys removed her coat and placed it on the hook by the door. She stood close to the fire, but waited to sit until Mrs. Davis suggested it, which didn't take long.

Mrs. Davis brought a steaming cup of coffee for

Gladys and one for herself and sat in the opposite chair. "It's been ages, dear. Catch me up on everything."

Gladys wasn't sure what to say. Her life wasn't exactly exciting. "I'm still getting along well with the children. We just planted some seeds that will be transplanted once the weather warms. I spent the holidays with the Crowley's and that was lovely."

"Oh, I'm glad to hear that. I was thinking about you hoping you were enjoying yourself. So, what brings you by today?"

Gladys took a sip of coffee to give herself a moment to think about how to approach the subject. "Well, I was hoping to see Mr. Davis. It's about a school matter."

"I'm sorry, but he isn't here and won't be for a while. He said he had a meeting after work and to expect him home late. Is there something that I can help you with or maybe I can pass a message along?"

The inside of Gladys cheek began to hurt as she chewed it. "I'm not sure. I suppose you could share my concerns with him. See, Mr. Ulinski is lighting the fire for me each morning. I'm not there mind you, nothing improper is taking place. He stopped by a few weeks ago showing concern for me as my walk in the snow leaves me cold and wet to start my day."

"Oh, dear. That sounds miserable. I hadn't realized it. I do apologize."

"No need. I signed up for this. It comes with the job and I do love the job, "she rushed to add.

Mrs. Davis sighed. "I'm glad to hear that, dear. Is that all? I'm sure Mr. Davis won't mind him lighting your fire."

Gladys suddenly looked very uncomfortable. "I wish that was all. Earlier today, Mr. Crowley brought us soil for our seed planting. Miss Siller came out after he left and said something to me that left me concerned and uncomfortable."

Mrs. Davis stood and began pacing. "What did she say?"

Her pacing only increased Gladys's uneasy feeling. She really wanted to be settled into life here by now. Changing houses monthly and not having many friends was taking its toll on her. She didn't want to get Miss Siller in trouble, but she herself wanted to stay out of it and Gladys didn't know what else to do.

If she could figure out how to win over the other teachers, she was sure everything else would settle into place. The information the Kemp's gave her left little hope for that. "She told me to be careful and said she would hate for Mr. Davis to have to let me go."

Mrs. Davis paused and turned to face her. "How dare she! You have been a joyful addition to our community. I cannot say the same for the other two."

Gladys was confused. If she was so loved, but the others weren't, why did the town seem to avoid her, but flock to them? "I was just hoping to share this with Mr. Davis so he was aware should any news reach his ears."

"Well, I will be happy to pass along the information." Under her breath she added, "And deal with Miss Siller."

"Thank you, ma'am. Do you by any chance know where I am moving to?"

Mrs. Davis was lost in thought for a moment but shook her head back to the present. "Uh, yes I believe it's with the Kilpatrick's."

Gladys closed her eyes. She would take anyone but them. Apparently, Mrs. Davis understood her facial expression.

"We only have a handful of families able to do rotations with you. They are one who has volunteered for multiple opportunities. Mr. Davis is trying to space out your stays with them as much as possible, though."

Gladys supposed she was to be thankful for that. Being thankful for anything concerning the Kilpatrick's was trying. "Thank you for your hospitality." She raised her mug of coffee before setting it on the nearest table and retrieving her coat.

"Are you leaving so soon, dear?"

Gladys just wanted to flee after hearing that news. She had thought she was having a bad day, but it was nothing compared to what the days ahead would bring. "I'm afraid so. I have some things to attend to before supper tonight."

"As do I. Thank you for stopping and I'll be sure to pass along the information."

Mrs. Davis walked her to the door and saw her out. Gladys walked slowly with a new pressing weight on her shoulders. A few good days and moments she shared with a handful of lovely people didn't make up for the miserable days in between. She did want this to work, but if things didn't turn around soon, she wasn't sure how.

CHAPTER 26

*M*icha was settling in at work and was finally starting to feel like he under- stood the ins and outs of the electrical portion of the mine. Thankfully, nothing serious had occurred that required his attention as he didn't think he was yet qualified for that. The everyday goings on were easy enough, though, and Micha worked side-by-side with the senior engineer. He knew someday soon that would change and he would be required to run the operation solo.

Just when Micha thought the day would go without a hitch the pump lost power. Micha threw some switches to no avail. The next step was to head to the pumps and see if the problem could be spotted at that end. He quickly made his way to Mr. Davis and the pumps. Any issue of this size would halt work in the mine and the bosses would not be happy about that.

"Afternoon, Charles," Micha greeted, then set in inspecting the wiring going to the pump while Mr. Davis was fiddling with the controls of the pump itself.

Finding the issue didn't take very long. A frayed wire was spotted and repaired quickly, setting all back into motion. Micha was ready to head back and let Mr. Davis continue with his job when he was stopped.

"Hey, Micha. Hold up a minute." Mr. Davis walked around the machinery and stopped in front of Micha with his arms crossed. "I've wanted to talk to you but haven't found the time to spare. Can you stay a minute or two?"

Micha wasn't sure what Mr. Davis would need from him. He also wasn't sure why he was feeling a bit antsy. "I think I can."

"Good, good. How's the house going for you? It's far different from the company house."

Now Micha was concerned. He loved his private home. Lady was doing well and Micha refused to give her up. Sure, it was a bit lonely at times, but he would take that over all the ribbing from the guys any day. If Micha was honest, he didn't like the single lifestyle. The company house was wild at times. A party now and again was fine, but drinking nightly was not his idea of fun.

"I really like living there. I like the peace and quiet. Lady enjoys it."

"Ah yes, Lady. Miss Wimble has been cleaning for you. Is she still?"

Micha did not know where this conversation was going. "Yes. She is there once a week while I'm working."

"I do wonder how she can manage her full-time work and this part time. She seems to be keeping it all together and doing well though."

"Uh, yes." Micha wasn't sure what Mr. Davis was wanting from him. "She enjoys the kids. I don't think she thinks of that job as a job. She really loves working there."

Mr. Davis looked at Micha a while, which left Micha feeling nervous. "I wonder what she is doing with all of her pay?" It wasn't a question directed to Micha, merely a statement.

"She's saving it. Miss Wimble would like her own place and she is working at being able to pay for that." Why Micha felt the need to answer the statement was beyond him. He attributed it to his nervousness.

Mr. Davis narrowed his eyes. "You seem to know a lot about her. Especially given that you say you don't see her, as she cleans when you are away here."

Micha pulled at his shirt collar. He suddenly was feeling like it was choking him. "We see each other in passing."

"Yes, I see. And I know you are building her fire each day. All of this combined with our last conversation got me to thinking. Are you smitten for the teacher?"

Micha started to cough. He seemed to be choking. Mr. Davis began hitting his back a bit and he was laughing. "No, sir. I just don't like when someone is struggling and I can do something about it. Especially when that someone is female."

Mr. Davis nodded, but kept a silly grin on his face. "Son, you can argue it all you want, but it's clear as day written all over your face."

Micha was stunned speechless.

"I do need you to remember that she has signed a contract. There are certain rules she must follow to remain in good standing with the school. Now, if you want to court her that is fine, as long as you do it properly. You may not be alone with her. Crossing paths in the street is fine, but in the school or at your home you need to make sure that you don't compromise her. Unfortunately, we have some individuals here who seem to not care for her. They seem to be sitting and waiting for opportunities to pounce to get her in trouble. If you like her as much as I think you do, I need your help to keep her protected."

"Yes, sir." Micha wasn't ready to admit that Mr. Davis was right. Micha had been kidding himself for months now, but he wouldn't say it out loud. He knew Mr. Davis was right in his assumptions.

"Good man." Mr. Davis turned back to his machine. "Oh, and Micha, baseball meetings on Saturday. I want you on my team. You're playing this year."

"Yes, sir!" That Micha could agree with. He loved baseball and looked forward to it every year. It gave him something to do that wasn't drinking with the guys. Or worse, playing cards and losing his wages. "I'm excited for baseball season this year."

"Good, glad to hear it. We've got some stiff competition again." The surrounding towns each had teams and baseball games became rivalries between towns and miners or loggers. It gave the men some- thing to do besides work. It was a way to work out frustrations and build friendships.

Micha's head spun as he walked back to the control panel. He wasn't exactly sure what happened with that conversation, but now he knew he couldn't lie to himself anymore. He really cared for Gladys. He didn't know what it was about her. He certainly didn't think this would happen when he had first met her.

Gladys had her defenses up, but sometime over the course of the last months she had dropped those and began to show her true self. She really loved what she did, and the kids were everything to her. She was focused and determined.

Gladys certainly did not have many friends here, but she seemed to keep her head held high and focused on her goal. All these things solidified how proud Micha was of her. And now, yes, he was admitting that it made him like her as well. How deep the like went was hard to say. Now that he was willing to admit it, he could begin to think about what he was going to do about it.

This new revelation left Micha flustered for the remainder of the day. Focusing on his work was trying. He kept getting lost in his thoughts. Micha had never liked anyone before. Not in this way, anyway. He wasn't sure what this meant or what would happen next. He also wanted to know how

Gladys felt, but he refused to come out and talk to her.

She was scholarly, and Micha couldn't read. Gladys probably didn't have any feelings for him in that way. Micha was a means for her finding a permanent home. That also meant she would no longer be a teacher. He wondered what her main goal was. Would she give up teaching to have a home? Would that be enough to be with him?

Micha sighed and shoved all thoughts away. Spinning in circles would answer nothing. He decided just to keep doing what he was doing, but to start paying more attention to her - what she was saying, asking her questions. He needed to know her better.

CHAPTER 27

*G*ladys was not at all happy about moving back in with the Kilpatrick's. Knowing the routine and what was to be expected ahead of time helped ease the transition a bit. The one positive she could find with this situation was she had her own bed, albeit in the main room. Not sharing a bed like she did at many other homes, besides the Kemp's, where she had her own room, she was able to sleep better.

Another bright spot staying with the Kilpatrick's would be Sarah. She helped make the days pass more quickly. Given her position at the school, she and Sarah could not be true friends. Gladys was in authority over Sarah. While she was still in school, they would need to keep that distance. After school,

Gladys could see herself and Sarah becoming great friends. Gladys was preparing breakfast with Sarah, catching up with each other's lives.

"I met a boy."

Gladys stopped mid kneading. "You what?"

Sarah giggled. "Well, he really is a man, not a boy. He is a logger, not a miner. I could never fall for a miner. And his name is Paul."

Maybe it wasn't as serious as she was thinking. Gladys hoped it wasn't anyway. "This is probably just an infatuation. You are a young girl noticing boys." She made sure to call this person a boy and not a man to further stick her point. "It's normal for your age. I'm sure you will have several in your sights before it's time to settle down, if it ever is. Maybe you'll want to be a teacher like me when you're grown up."

"Oh no, teaching is not for me. Of course, I've never had a teacher like you. All of mine have been grumpy. And Paul is a man. He's been working now for two years and will be eighteen soon."

Gladys was quickly reaching a panic level and she wasn't even sure why. Sarah was not her child. Gladys shouldn't care, should she? She was old enough to be married even if Gladys didn't agree with it. The teacher in her wanted all the students to finish school. Before Gladys could say anything more Mrs. Kilpatrick entered the kitchen.

"Tsk tsk, why are the biscuits not in the oven yet?"

Gladys took a deep, calming breath before answering, "Sorry ma'am. Sarah and I were having a conversation and it slowed me down."

"And what pray be important enough to delay breakfast?" Mrs. Kilpatrick was glaring at her daughter.

"Yes, Momma, I was just telling Miss Wimble about Paul." Sarah looked to Miss Wimble with nervous eyes. Mrs. Kilpatrick looked between the girls. "That is not a discussion to be having during preparations for breakfast. You may talk about it on the walk to school if you can finish in time."

"Yes, ma'am," they both said in unison and looked at each other. Gladys resumed her kneading with a fervor. And the girls remained silent for the remainder of breakfast preparations.

The walk to school was still cold, but the snow had begun to melt, which meant spring was soon around the corner.

Gladys' dress was soggier than before due to the snow melting. The cotton petticoats seemed to wick up water extremely fast and her wool overlayer did not provide adequate insulation. It would take her half the day to fully warm up even with the fire being already built.

Her walks were no longer lonely in addition to being miserable. She now had Sarah. Sarah didn't have to walk with her as she, being a student, wasn't required to arrive as early as Gladys was. But she was grateful for the company.

"Your mother didn't say anything regarding our conversation earlier."

Gladys was trying to delicately pull more information out of Sarah that could help her understand Sarah's desires, and hopefully find a way to redirect her path.

"Sarah you do realize that this is a permanent decision, right? Once you leave school and marry that's it. You don't get to be a girl anymore. You will then be required to run a home and prepare for future children."

Sarah thought about that quietly for a moment before responding. "I do. I've always wanted to be married and getting out of my home would be a relief. I'm already taking care of a home and children with the amount of work Momma leaves for me. Paul is a wonderful man and treats me very well. He has come to dinner a few times and understands through those times and gossip talk around town about how my family is, and he is still around. He hasn't run. Most boys won't even look at me for fear of my momma. Momma is a tough woman and holds deep hurts. I really think she still mourns my father and in some strange way blames us kids. I really feel like her work that she pushes on us is a form of punishment for her loss."

Gladys had tears in her eyes from listening to this child. The whole situation was terribly sad and although she didn't agree with Sarah marrying so young, she could at least understand the desire a bit more. "Sarah, I'm so sorry you've not had the easiest life. I want you to promise me something. Please take your time. Don't rush into this decision, because once it's done, it can't be undone."

"I do understand that. I have no intention of wanting to undo it."

Gladys smiled softly at her statement.

"Does anyone usually get married wanting to be unbound before the I do's are said?"

Gladys paused thinking about that question herself. She supposed there could be a few reasons for that instance to come up, but overall, she felt that was not the case. And there in lay the reason she wanted to teach. She knew her future. It was all laid out for her.

Sure, the where's and who's could change at any given time, but teaching was something she could rely on forever. Being married to her job meant no one could fall out of love with her. She didn't have to depend or rely on anyone but herself. Her happiness was hers for the taking, not reliant upon another.

"I don't want to undo a marriage once I'm in one." Sarah tried to reassure her.

"Oh, I'm sure you don't. But do you really know what this Paul is thinking? How do you know you can trust him to be there for you and with you forever?"

Sarah thought deeply and stopped walking altogether. "I can't. I don't think anyone truly can for the sole reason that no one knows when their time on Earth is done. Even the closest loving marriages can end in the blink of an eye, leaving a once very happy and well-provided for lady left to fend for herself."

Sarah was wise, and Gladys was not prepared for it. "Maybe I've underestimated you. You are so young yet, but you've had to grow up faster than others. Please, don't rush. And really, work to get to know him as much as you can first."

"That I can promise." The two hugged and began

walking again. "I can't wait for you to meet him."

"I look forward to that day. And I will give you an honest opinion about him after," she added as they walked into the school. Sarah and Gladys parted to go to each of their rooms. Gladys wished her a great day full of learning and to cram as much as possible in her brain before she left school forever. Sarah smiled and nodded.

Upon entering the classroom she moved close to the fire and worked briefly to take the biggest chills away. She was very thankful for Micha and all his help. Gladys looked around the room and wondered if she loved this enough to really last her full life or if this was just meant for right now. Was marriage still a part of her future despite earlier thoughts of it never being a part of her?

She sighed as she noticed the flowers that had been about half grown already. Most of them were limp, discolored, and quite sad-looking. Gladys panicked and began watering them, hoping maybe that was the cause. She soon realized lack of water was not the problem. The plants had frozen.

Moving as many as she could closer to the fire, she tried to think of how it happened, but there was no sign of anything that could have done this. It was still cold outside, and it did get cold in the room, but it was no longer cold enough to freeze them inside. Immediately her thoughts went to who could have done it and she chastised herself. Would the old Gladys, pointing fingers and wanting revenge, never truly go away? She was left with those thoughts when the children began arriving.

Gladys was sad to tell her class that some, if not all, of their plants would die. Trying to soften the hurt, she made certain to tell them she would bring more seeds and they could start again. Many kids took it in stride, but a few of them still cried. Gladys was unsure of what to do, but an idea popped into her head.

"Class, just as soon as the snow melts more and the spring wildflowers begin to emerge from the ground, we will have a field trip."

Shouts and hollers filled the room and she tried to quiet them down quickly. Her idea made her feel excited, too. Getting out to see the natural fauna and flora was already on her to do list. She wasn't sure why she hadn't thought of taking the kids with her before.

And just like that, a most certain rotten day became sunny. Gladys was slowly learning how to make her own happiness instead of using the hurt and pain from others for it.

CHAPTER 28

*G*ladys knew that baseball was important. She knew that by all the buzz about the upcoming season and how many were eager and willing to get out and work in the still cold conditions. They waited until the snow had completely melted to begin preparations, but they were antsy while they waited.

Sylvia had explained that each year was different. Some winters the snow melted in March and other years they had to wait until May before getting the field ready.

This year they were lucky it seemed. They only had to wait until early April for the complete melt. Games would start toward the end of May and run through the summer. Gladys wasn't all that excited about baseball, but crocus had begun popping up through the mud here and there and she was happy to see some wild blooms. In a few weeks' time, she supposed, the underbrush would have enough growth for their field trip.

Gladys was watching her students working in what she was told was called the diamond. The mine approved of the games and supported them, allowing a few workers at a time off early to work on the field. Each class took their turn donating hours for the cause as well. Her students, being the youngest, were tasked with weed pulling.

Weeds seem to be the first to sprout as soon as the ground was soft enough for them. Flowers took their sweet time. Gladys pondered as she watched her students and pointed out the differences between weeds and flowers.

Scientifically they were all plants, each with their own unique structures, but why were some classified as weed and other flower? Weeds seem to be easier to grow and multiply. Flowers took a gentle hand, were particular to their soil and water amount, and some- times needed a bit of coaxing to bloom.

Her students were similar: some of them were gung-ho and ready to jump into everything while others took their time and needed praise and encouragement. Did that mean one type of student was preferred to the other? Not to her. Each was different and unique in their own right.

This all drew Gladys to another comparison. No one wanted the weeds. They pulled and pulled to keep gardens rid of them. People could be like that as well. Some no one wanted around. They would cross the street or change their complete destination to avoid them.

Gladys knew this first-hand and it hurt. She and her mother could be called weeds. She didn't want that. She knew some flowers growing up - people who everyone flocked to. It seemed the flowers always had friends hovering around and usually those friends were also flowers. The weeds kept together, and many times turned on each other, fighting for more land. Gladys really wanted to be a flower. But could a weed become a flower?

Looking up to check on her students and pulling herself out of her thoughts, she noticed Micha was making his way to her or towards her, at least.

"Good afternoon, Miss Wimble." Micha sat next to her but kept space and used the formal way to address her for propriety reasons.

Gladys glanced his way and felt warmer on this chilly day just from sitting next to him.

"You all right? You seem to be off in your own world."

Gladys turned back to the kids. "Oh yes, yes I'm fine. Good morning."

Micha was positive she was lying to him. The look on her face as he walked over was concerning enough without the sad tone to her voice and deep thoughts going on about something.

Not wanting to talk to him about flowers and weeds she quickly thought of something to say. "What are we doing here anyway? What is this game of baseball?"

Micha's eyebrows couldn't have climbed higher on his forehead. "You don't know what baseball is?"

Gladys gave a nervous laugh. "Well, no, not really. I know you have a stick and a ball."

Now it was Micha's turn to chuckle. "The stick is actually a bat and it's used to hit the ball. If you do hit it, you get to run the bases."

"Those white things out there?"

"Yes, those are the bags or bases. If you can get around all of them and back to where you started without getting out, you give your team a point."

She scrunched up her nose. "Only one point. But there are four bases out there. Shouldn't you get four points?"

Micha full-on laughed at that. "I do like the way you think. Sometimes it's easy to run all those and other times getting a point for each would feel better about all the work it took for your team to get you home."

"Wait, your team gets you home? But I thought you did that by running the bases."

Micha realized he needed to step back a bit. He started from the beginning and went into detail explaining the basics to her.

Gladys wasn't sure she followed all of that and hadn't realized it was as complicated as Micha made it sound. Men with balls and sticks, or bats, she thought was silly. Maybe she had misjudged a bit too soon. That was weed behavior. Flowers would take the time to understand before they held an opinion.

"Thanks for bringing the kids out here today. They are a big help," Micha offered.

Gladys already knew that. She had a great group and would be sad to see her older ones move up at the end of the year. "I'm happy they could help. I hope they did enough."

"They did. The diamond should be free of all weeds with nice crisp edges. Weeding is an ongoing process that we all must work on throughout the season to keep the field in tip top shape."

Weeding is an ongoing process.

She knew that was important for her but couldn't make sense of it. "Well, let me know if you would like their help again. Getting the kids outside the more the weather heats up is good for them."

"I think we are good, but I will let you know if they are needed. Really the older kids can do more. Not to mean your students are not helpful. It's just the older kids can naturally do more."

Gladys smiled. "I understand. They do try their best." She looked back at her kids who were mostly working. A few of them had begun drawing in the dirt with sticks. "Well, most of them try to do their best, anyway."

They both laughed. Micha stood. "It was nice talking to you. Have a great day Miss Wimble."

Gladys watched Micha walk back to the field, engaging with the kids as he passed them. She desperately wanted to be a flower. This weed business was lonely and apparently produced a smell everyone else noticed but her. She figured that out because she had been sitting there for over an hour and Micha was the only adult to approach her. Everyone else kept their distance, like they were afraid her stench would waft onto them.

With a sigh, Gladys stood and called her children

over. She decided to dismiss them home from there. One look at how dirty they were from rolling around in the dirt meant she either could release them early or she'd have extra cleaning in her room.

The kids jumped and squealed at her words. It was only less than an hour before they would normally be sent home, but they either didn't know or didn't care. To them early was early and they loved it. She just hoped the parents were not going to be upset with her for not only letting them go home early, but also the caked in dirt on their clothing.

CHAPTER 29

*G*ladys woke up excited. It was a beautiful spring day. The sun was rising quickly in the sky and the rays brought the warmth that seeped into one's bones. It wasn't hot yet, as in the summer months, but warm enough to not need heavy layers through the whole day. The sounds of birds and other wildlife beginning to frolic in delight only added to the brilliance of the day.

The children didn't know, but she did. She thought surprising them the day of the field trip was better. Of course, they already knew they would be going, they just were not sure when that would be. They also didn't know where they would be going.

After settling the children upon their arrival, she

informed them of her plans. They screamed in delight and she quickly worked to quieten them down so the other two classes were not disturbed.

They were to take their lunches, and Gladys' plans were to look for a suitable lunch spot to enjoy an outside picnic. Gladys had noticed the vast amounts of berry bushes and, although she enjoyed the fruits they would again provide, she dearly hoped they could find a bit of grass to sit on instead of having to stand or fear getting stabbed by briars or having their clothing snagged by them.

After the children grabbed their lunches that were brought to school each day in various tins, they were off. The trail they started up was the one leading directly to the mine. Once at the mine they would branch off on another trail she had spied earlier when she scoped out the surroundings.

She had traveled up to the mine before, never getting too close, but close enough to take it all in. That was how she knew about the other trails. Not yet traveling those before meant she was just as excited as the children for this adventure.

Many of the children had come as far as the mine. Some of them excitedly told her stories of getting to go into parts of it with their fathers. None of them had been in the deepest parts and she was happy to hear that.

Once she directed them onto the next trail she discovered that none of them had traveled beyond the mine itself. Gladys wanted to instill a love of nature within them all and she hoped this little hike would do just that.

As the forest enclosed around them and the trail, she instructed her students to be on the lookout for any and all flowers. She wanted them to point them out to her should she miss seeing them first. That meant looking in all directions as they traveled further along the trail and away from the mine.

The children quickly obliged. They were excited and those found included dying Easter lilies, other lilies she wasn't sure the name of, dandelions, asters, clovers, and even more she wasn't sure exactly which flower families they belonged to.

The underbrush was a beautiful easel of a variety of colors. Unfortunately, Gladys knew wildflowers generally were more fragile than the flowers grown in gardens. She would have loved to pick many to make a big bouquet, but chances were, they would all be wilted by the time she made it to a vase with water.

Wildlife abounded as well. The numbers of birds

and small animals they saw were numerous. The sounds of the forest soothed and relaxed her. The children delighted in the sightings of bunnies and field mice.

Finding a meadow turned out to not be as difficult as she initially thought. The forest wasn't closed as she first thought from viewing it before entering. There were several open areas where the sun spread through and brought more splashes of color than in the shadows of the trees.

The kids were clearly very hungry from the excursion. She also used that time to quiz the students, making sure they were not only enjoying this outing, but also learning about their own backyards.

After everyone finished eating and she felt they had a decent idea of the plant life around them, she decided to turn back and head for home.

Gladys thought back over the relaxing and glorious day as they walked. It's why she couldn't fathom how it turned terrifying. Her mind replayed all the events, seeking a turning moment that she had missed. Some small warning before the confusion. She stood with most of her students surrounding her, eyes wide with fright, looking to her for what to do next and she had no idea.

She kept replaying the day, such a wonderful, beautiful day. Gladys couldn't comprehend how that turned into a nightmare. A student was missing, another few were sent ahead running to find help. Gladys was frozen, standing in the trail, not sure which direction to move.

CHAPTER 30

icha took off running at a speed he only used in baseball. He had been above ground when he saw the children appear out of the woods. It struck him as odd, wondering what they were doing at that time of day there. He watched them as they ran closer. It didn't take long to see that all of them were running from something, or to something, and one was crying. Micha had picked up his pace after seeing that and got to the children before they made it to the mine.

Micha wanted them to just spit out what it was but because they were so upset, it took several attempts before the right words in the right order were spoken. Once they did it took him a moment to believe what they said. None of it made any sense.

He sent the kids on to the mine to find more help and Micha had taken off to town. He did not want to be the one to break this kind of news, but for some reason there he was on his way to tell a mother her daughter was missing.

By the time he reached town, he was out of breath and dirty from where he had taken a spill after tripping on a rock. He was glad only his pants got dirty and his skin was a bit scraped up. That fall could have ended much worse. Of course, not being able to walk due to a broken leg would have meant he wouldn't have to destroy one of the nicest women this town had.

Bracing himself and taking a deep breath, Micha knocked on the door. It didn't take long for the curious but warm and generous eyes to land on him only to change quickly to fright.

"Oh, tell me it's not James." Mrs. Crowley's hand had flown to her heart to keep it from fluttering right out of her chest.

"No, no. Nothing like that ma'am. Please, can I come in?"

SYLVIA WAS VERY CONCERNED, as Micha wasn't around during the day most days. Knowing that James was all right though did help to calm her nerves. "Well, it's not someone else at the mine then? Is my assistance required for some reason?"

Micha remained quiet and the silence only intensified Sylvia's concern. He quickly added that everything at the mine was in tip top shape and all was well to reduce her fears.

"Well, then I don't seem to understand what has brought you here today with a look of disgust or perhaps pain. You are feeling well, aren't you? Oh, I can put on some tea, or fix you a poultice if you are feeling poorly."

"No, ma'am, it's nothing like that. I have something to tell you but I'd feel a bit better if you were sitting first."

Sylvia did not understand all this drama over whatever Micha felt she needed to know. James was fine, the mine was fine. She had sent Jeffrey and Sadie off to school like normal and if something were amiss there, one of the teachers or older students would have come for her. The school was in the opposite direction of the mine, so Micha couldn't be connected that way. She sat to ease Micha's worries, but felt it was a bit unnecessary.

Micha began pacing back and forth. "So, I'm not sure on all the details. And the children that told me were quite worked up so it could be simply a misunderstanding. I'm actually sure all is well now, and they are all on their way back to town."

Sylvia's head was swimming. "Children told you? Back to town? Micha you are not making any sense. Why were there children up at the mine with you? Unless you weren't working today?"

"No, I was working. I saw them first running towards help. Ma'am, Sadie is missing."

Sylvia's face went from confusion to a look that had never crossed her face before.

Sylvia stood and wobbled a bit before finding her footing . "What do you mean missing? She is at school with the rest of the children."

Micha was pacing faster now. "See, that's what I can't understand. A group of kids ran out of the woods and said that Sadie was missing. I can't figure out what they were doing on that deer trail in the first place. And if only Sadie was missing, does that mean it was only them and her? Where is the class? How did Miss Wimble not know they left the school?"

Sylvia began pacing herself, trying to put it all together. It didn't take long for a conversation with

Sadie and Jeffrey to enter her mind from a few weeks back. "The nature hike!"

"The what?"

"That nature hike. Gladys was teaching the class about botany. She had a field trip in the works to take them on a little nature hike. It must have been today."

"But she doesn't know the area. How did she know where to go or that it would be safe?" He turned and was staring at Sylvia, opened mouthed. "And we have hungry bears this time of year just waiting for an easy meal."

Sylvia fell back at that and Micha spoke a curse word. He quickly helped her up and to a chair before running out of the house yelling back, "Don't you worry, ma'am. We will find her safe and sound."

CHAPTER 31

*B*y quitting time, only the other students and Miss Wimble had returned to town. Sylvia had twice walked up the hill to the mine just to be sent back home to wait.

Micha knew that had to be aggravating. With no searchers back, he decided to head to Miss Wimble and get the story from her. Maybe she would give a clue that he could use to find Sadie before dark.

Miss Wimble was hard to track down. She wasn't at the school, nor at her current residence. He checked the store before finally making his way to The Crowley's. Truth be told, he didn't want to show up there again without good news. He needed to speak with Gladys, so he found himself knocking on their door for a second time in the same day.

"Hello again, ma'am. I'm looking for Miss Wimble."

Sylvia didn't say a word. She simply just opened the door further to allow Micha to see Gladys sitting by the fire, her face drained of all color despite the warm fire burning close beside her.

Micha stepped in and took a seat across from Gladys. He watched her for a minute before finally asking her to tell him the events of the day. She did almost as if by rote. She said them, matter of fact, and as if she had been repeating it frequently. Micha supposed she had. He knew he would if he was the one in charge and came home short. He thanked her and took his leave with an idea to try.

"I'M SO SORRY."

"Gladys, you keep saying that and I need you to stop. I know you are sorry. I'm not blaming you. I knew about the trip and had no issue with it. Sadie is the one at fault here."

Gladys fiddled with a wet handkerchief that had been soaking up frightened tears. "I don't know how you are so calm. I'm a nervous wreck."

"I'm not calm. Inside I'm a mess, but I'm working

to remember that God is in control. He knows where she is, and I have faith that He will lead someone to her in time. I know that James is up there searching, and I know he won't come home without her. I'm holding onto that to keep me going for now."

Gladys dabbed fresh tears. "I just don't understand. I want her home. I'd do anything to bring her home." She blew her nose. "I'm such a weed."

"You're a what?" Sylvia moved to sit in the chair Micha vacated.

"I'm a weed. You're a flower. Alice is a flower. I'm a weed no one wants and causes chaos and destruction everywhere I go. You should run from me. I'll keep taking more and more of your space until eventually you'll die."

Sylvia burst into full out laughter and Gladys glared at her. "Oh honey, thank you for that. I needed to laugh." She placed a hand on Gladys. "You are not a weed. Whatever put that idea into your head in the first place? Weeds are weeds and flowers are flowers. You are a person. People can behave like weeds or like flowers and the best part of it all is they can change between the two. And who is Alice anyway?"

Gladys wrinkled up her nose. "She's just a girl. A

girl that has always been a magnificent flower standing tall and proud next to my disgusting weed. No, they can't. I was born a weed and despite all my efforts to make people like me and do the right thing I always end up the weed."

Sylvia knelt beside her and stroked her hair. "I know you're not a weed. Want to know how I know?"

Gladys nodded as she blew again.

"A weed would be sitting here worrying about losing her job over this instead of worrying about Sadie. A weed would do what she wanted without hoping the town would love her. A weed wouldn't give of herself every day to teach complete strangers."

"The other two teachers do it and they seem to be weeds too."

Sylvia laughed again. "Those teachers are weeds, but they aren't here because they want to be. They are here because towns like ours pay more. They have their own place and make more money being willing to live out here in the boonies than in the big city. Besides, if they truly loved and cared about the kids, they wouldn't have done to you what they did this past Christmas program. Your ideas were amazing, and they chose to be mean and rude as punishment to you. And what did you do? You rose to the occasion and put it on for the kids despite them. You are a flower through and through."

Gladys was confused. "But you said a weed is a weed and a flower is a flower. I can't change."

"No, I was saying they won't change. You are a person and a person can. They could, too, if they really wanted to. I don't think they do, but I know you do. You read Psalm one and tell me you are not a flower."

Sylvia let that sink into Gladys before continuing. "Now, Gladys, will you pray with me please?"

Gladys nodded, but was unable to speak. She let Sylvia say the prayer and Gladys felt it in her heart.

Afterwards, Sylvia posed a question to her. "Why do you think God allowed this job to open up for you?"

Gladys shrugged her shoulders.

"Do you think this is all just happenstance? I don't. I think you needed to be here, so you could grow into that flower. Back in Deer Lodge, you were restricted. Your petals couldn't open to show you that you are indeed a flower and not a weed. Your mother had a tight hold on you, not allowing them to open in the sun. Here you can."

Is it really God's will that she was here?

Gladys wasn't sure, but that did give her something to ponder.

DARK WAS APPROACHING QUICKLY and Micha was anxious to find little Sadie. He made one stop on his way back up to the mine and onto the trail. It was to his home to grab a lantern and Lady. Micha wasn't sure if Lady would know what to do or not, but he felt it was worth a try. Lady loved Sadie and if she was meant to use her nose for finding anyone, he knew it would be her.

Lady ran up ahead of Micha and he struggled to keep up. He knew he needed to, as come dark, it would be harder to see her too far up ahead.

They passed some men returning with no luck. Micha pushed forward following Lady to a clearing where Lady stopped a moment. It gave Micha a chance to catch up. Lady spun in a few circles and jumped excitedly as in play. After a minor scolding for playing he spoke firm to her reminding her of what mission they were on. Micha didn't really think Lady understood him, but maybe she would understand the seriousness of them being out there by his tone.

After the clearing, Lady took Micha on a hike through the brush. He moved quickly to keep up which caused sticks underneath to snap and him to get caught a couple of times in bushes.

The underbrush was very thick off the deer trail.

If Micha didn't know how to track he could easily get turned around. Lady started barking and making a fuss causing Micha to pick up his pace. Once he reached the dog he realized she had found a bedded down fawn.

His heart was racing from the speed to get there and he hoped that Sadie had been found, but after he saw the little deer his heart plummeted in disappointment. He still praised Lady for finding something, though. Maybe that would encourage her to keep trying to find what he wanted.

It was after they had started again, he realized somewhere in all the hustle he had torn his pants. They were split clear open at his right thigh. He also had a nasty scrape that was bleeding. Most likely that meant he pushed through the blackberry briars without even realizing it. The barbs on those bushes were large and stocky. The thorns, or in these parts some called them prickers, were soft when they were small, but as they grew, they became about as hard as a tree branch itself. And they were nasty, too, slicing the flesh of the strongest of men. Micha felt lucky, as it appeared the pricker didn't break off and embed into his flesh.

It wasn't long after they began again that Micha started hearing grunting noises. He whispered as loud as he could to get Lady to stop while trying not to scare whatever it was up ahead. Lady had other plans however, and she picked up her pace, growling and barking full-steam towards the grunts.

In that moment he wished he had thought to bring his rifle, as he was certain the noise was nothing other than a bear. Now, he feared for Lady. One swipe from a bear bigger than a cub could send Lady flying.

Micha began shouting loudly to get Lady off the track. The bear's sounds intensified briefly before he heard brush breaking. By the time Micha caught up with Lady he was stunned at what his sweet girl did. The bear had climbed a tree and was now camped up in the tall branches, staring down at the teddy bear dog who was baying at the base keeping it in place. Micha wouldn't have believed it if he hadn't seen it himself.

He patted Lady's head and scratched her ears while praising her. It was when he stopped, he could hear a faint cry. Lady must have heard it too, as she was off again on the track. It didn't take long as the cry was coming from very close to where the bear was treed, and Micha was thankful. He scooped up little Sadie who was certainly cold but seemed to be unscathed, if not a bit scared. She curled into his arms not saying a word and the three of them turned, making their way back home with Lady trotting proudly, leading the way. In the distance they heard the sound of the enormous, yet agile, man-eating beast jump out of the tree and run off in the opposite direction. Micha had to hand it to her. Lady had earned her lifetime of keep in one night.

CHAPTER 32

*G*ladys disembarked the train, keeping eyes on the back of Sylvia so not to lose her. The crowd that gathered to meet the train was at least four people deep and longer than the train itself. She supposed many of those people were meeting loved ones as they trickled off, and yet others were waiting to board, their families waving them off.

Tacoma seemed busier than any other place she had been to, not that she had been many places. Gladys hadn't traveled beyond what was needed for her career.

Stepping out away from the crowd, Gladys was able to turn back and see the depot. Sylvia had stopped to take in the magnificence of the building. It held arches on all sides and the center rose higher and was capped with a dome. It was beautiful. Gladys had never seen a building that was also a work of art. She smiled and noticed Sylvia was smiling at the building, too.

"It sure is pretty, huh?"

"Yes, it sure is." She nodded and turned toward Sylvia. "Thank you again for letting me join you on this trip. I don't know why you did, though." She dropped her gaze to her feet.

Sylvia sighed. "Would you stop that, please? Quit beating yourself up for something you didn't do. Sadie took off on her own. She didn't tell you she was going, she just up and left, looking for more flowers. It's clearly a lesson she needed to learn. And quite frankly, I'm glad you didn't rob her of that lesson."

"Rob her of the lesson? I don't understand. I'm her teacher. I should have kept her close with my eyes on her at all times."

"Gladys, let's walk and talk. Every child needs to learn the dangers of this world. They need to get scared every once and again. If you took that opportunity away, there would have been a next time. She needed to learn it and it would have happened at some point again with potentially a different outcome."

"But this one could have been a different outcome."

Sylvia looked to the sky and took a deep breath. "Yes, you are right. It could have been, but it wasn't. She learned the lesson and ended up fine. If you protect them and coddle them the entire time, they will still grow up. You can't keep them little forever. These lessons and others must be learned now. See the bigger they get the bigger they will mess up. But now, Sadie, and Jeffrey by watching, have had the opportunity to make the mistake and learn from it. We shouldn't have this problem happen again, at least with those two." She patted her stomach to indicate the next bundle on its way.

Gladys thought about that for a while as they walked. Every time she made a mistake, her mother either made excuses for it or changed the story and said it to anyone and everyone she passed. Gladys' mistakes would mean her mother would be looked down upon, or so her mother thought. Perhaps that was why she, as an adult, still seemed to make errors in judgment when dealing with others. It could possibly be why she would jump to conclusions and judge first before stopping to think. That's what she was taught to do. Maybe she wasn't truly a weed trying to morph into a flower, but a flower all along who was taught to be a weed. She sighed and changed the subject.

"Sylvia, what is your family like? Not the four of you, I mean your extended families. I just realized you know much about me, but I haven't really taken the time to get to know your history. That was wrong of me and I'm sorry." Sylvia was always helping Gladys. She guided her when needing, but never released anything onto her. Gladys had much to learn when it came to true friendship, but this step felt like an important first one.

"Oh, it's all right. You are still trying to find your place. And we have talked some about me, but I know your mind and heart are busy working on settling in. I'm sure changing homes every month is making that all the harder to feel settled and at home. I do hope a solution can be figured out soon. And before I tell you my story, I hope you know you are now a part of the family. Once you're in, it's hard to get out. I hope you know that." Sylvia chuckled a bit after saying that.

Gladys' heart could all but burst with happiness from what she heard. She loved the Crowley's and loved thinking she was a part of them. She wasn't sure what her mother would think of that, but did her opinion matter?

She suddenly felt as though her mother's love was never at any point real love and she questioned what it made her and their relationship. For a true mother loves her children through the lessons of growing up, no matter how awkward or disappointed she feels. She certainly doesn't try to alter them for the betterment of herself.

Sylvia spent the next several minutes of their walk talking about her and Mr. Crowley's childhoods.

Gladys learned Mr. Crowley came from a very large family of seven. He was closest to his brother just older than him by a year. That brother currently lived in Indiana and tried with every letter to get them to move back East.

Mr. Crowley liked his job and the town. His reply would always be if anything ever changed, Indiana would be their next destination.

Mining towns were notorious for being dirty cities and mining bosses cruel. Ravensdale was different. The boss was strict, of course, and pay was meager, but the people who lived and worked together made it a great community to live in and grow a family. It was the exception to the norm and he didn't want to leave it for fear he wouldn't get it back.

Sylvia was one of four, all boys but her. Her father had died several years ago, her mother passed about a year back, and the boys were spread out living their own lives. She was never particularly close with any of them.

The trip to Tacoma was to purchase some things needed for the new baby that the company store didn't stock. They had everything needed, but when you wanted a certain color or pattern in fabric, you had to seek it elsewhere. The local store held the necessities and basics. They had material that the miners would need for their clothing and they also had some premade clothing. For the ladies, color was slim-pickings. Judging by what some of the ladies of the town wore, Gladys knew many of them made at least yearly trips to Tacoma to purchase material for themselves. There were, of course, many others who just made do with what could be found locally.

After they purchased what Sylvia came for, they found a delicatessen on their walk back to the depot and enjoyed a sandwich with a spot of tea to wash it down.

Gladys felt this was one of the best days in her

life and she was warmed to know that a huge thing as losing her child couldn't put a rift between her and her friend. Before today she was certain she had lost the only real friend she had made. After, she knew she had gained a family.

CHAPTER 33

Summer arrived and Gladys welcomed the warm long days, noisy birds chirping, and finally the feeling of belonging that settled over her. What she missed was her children. Summer meant school was out.

Of course, she saw many of them every day as she strolled through town, but it wasn't the same. She didn't have them all under one roof to enjoy for hours.

Having time on her hands meant she could work longer and more frequently for Micha. Instead of just cleaning, she decided to decorate it a bit. She had the thought before but didn't have the time. Now she had time to spare.

Most of the mining houses were sparse, with just

the minimal furnishings and little to no comfort. She assumed he wouldn't want anything too frilly, so the company store materials would suit just fine.

Gladys had plans for some curtains and chair cushions on each dining chair with some accent pillows for the rocker. She also would love to make a quilt with matching pillows for his bed but didn't want to take on more than she was ready for. Sylvia had taught her a few things and she knew she would help her through this as well, but with Sylvia growing larger by the day she didn't want to put more work on her than she already had.

Gladys climbed the front steps and entered the company store unnoticed. The room was empty of people, although she could hear some noise from the back. The store was crammed with anything and everything one would need to set up a home. The only thing it seemed to lack was color.

As she was combing through the collection of fabrics the bell on the door jingled. Gladys looked up and noticed it was two ladies with one of her students in tow. She smiled at little Bonnie before looking back down at the fabrics.

"Good morning, Miss Wimble."

Gladys froze. The voice was not from Bonnie, but from one of the adults. Gladys was so used to being basically ignored, especially by the ladies of the community, that she momentarily didn't know what to do. She quickly pulled herself together for a quick response.

"It's a beautiful day, isn't it?"

The voice was different from the first. Gladys knew it meant both women were speaking to her. A puzzled look crossed her face.

"Oh, where are my manners? I'm Dorothy and this is Elinore, Bonnie's mother."

"Yes, I know. It's very nice to officially meet you." Gladys dropped the fabric she was fingering and stood dumbfounded, staring at them.

"I wanted to thank you for teaching Bonnie this past year. She absolutely loved school and can't wait to go back."

Gladys smiled back at Bonnie, "I'm so glad you enjoyed it. I had a great time with you as well."

"The fabric selections here are very bland, but I suppose they get the job done. Do you have a special project you are working on?" Dorothy was attempting small talk and Gladys didn't know what to do about it.

She blinked a few times before responding, "Yes, I do. I'm making a few items to make Mic, uh Mr. Ulinski's home a bit homier."

Both ladies looked at each other. "Well, I do suppose the colors fit perfectly for a single man's home. We'll let you get back to it. Take care, Miss Wimble."

She followed them with her eyes as they moved into another aisle. Still dumbfounded, she randomly selected two fabrics and took them to the counter. She paid and walked out, the sunshine feeling glorious on her skin.

A new page had certainly turned for her. It wasn't until after she left, she thought to second guess what she had told them. It was the truth of course, but she couldn't help but wonder what those ladies would think and what they would share. Chastising herself for thinking of the negative instead of focusing on the positive, she shook her head and continued.

Gladys thought back through the past almost year in Ravensdale. She came knowing no one, frightened and nervous, but excited to be on her own. Her contract was officially up. She only signed on for a year.

Gladys knew a decision had to be made soon and Mr. Davis, most likely, would be seeking out her answer. She thought she knew what she should do before Sadie disappeared.

Going back to her mother was not a great solution and Gladys was positive her mother would use this experience to keep her from attempting any adult decision-making on her own in the future. Ironically, losing Sadie, she thought, was the final tipping point securing her fate, but it ended up proving the opposite.

Having the Crowley's in her life pulled her to stay. If she was being honest, they had a stronger pull than her mother did back home. Now that someone, or rather two people that she didn't temporarily live with, didn't flat out ignore her and tried to have an actual conversation with her increased the pull to stay here.

As she strolled back to Sylvia to show her the fabrics she'd selected and discuss patterns, she noticed the flowers that seemed to brighten the surroundings before now appeared to glow. She also realized part way there that she was skipping. Gladys hadn't skipped in several years. After chuckling a bit, she slowed her pace to a more ladylike walk.

"Well, aren't you chipper today?"

Sylvia was out front tending to the little flower garden her kids started for her. Gladys had given her a few more seeds to start and together they had separated some in the back garden and replanted up front. The little front yard shined proudly against the surrounding sparse ones.

"Good morning, I brought my fabrics over and was hoping you had a moment to help draw a pattern, so I can prepare the fabric." She held her hand out to help hoist Sylvia from the ground.

Sylvia raised an eyebrow to the fabrics. "You are planning on using those two together? I'm not sure they go."

Gladys truly looked down at them for the first time. She had chosen a rusty red color and mustard yellow. "At least they will brighten the place?"

Sylvia laughed. "That they will do. Come on. We'll get you started."

They ducked inside and laid out the red one on the table. Gladys told her she thought to make them into curtains. With his house being the exact same as the Crowley's, it made it much easier to measure, plot, and plan.

While they were working, she recapped her morning. Sylvia wasn't surprised like Gladys thought she would be. Apparently, she had known the town's feelings for her already.

"The people here are, mostly, good. It takes a while for people to trust, though. Then you add the other teachers doing their best to shape the overall opinion of you and it all chalks up to taking a bit longer than average. I'm sure many more will start to come around more often now."

Gladys was making notes when she stopped, unsure what Sylvia meant. "Why now? Has something changed?"

"You haven't heard? Why, yes something has changed. Something big. It seems that after a meeting with some of the prominent community members and top mine officials, plus Mr. Davis, an agreement was made to not continue the contracts of both Miss Dupont and Miss Siller."

Gladys' mouth couldn't open any farther. Her lower jaw hung at a very unladylike angle and Sylvia laughed before tapping on Gladys' chin. "We haven't had a teacher like you here before. The town decided we want to find more. Now we have two open positions to fill with, hopefully, better candidates."

Pacing back and forth, Gladys didn't know what to think. "Now they most certainly hate me. If they didn't before, this seals that."

"Oh, who really cares what they think." She waved her hand in the air as she said it and then smirked in Gladys' direction. "You are acting like a flower my dear. A weed would be jumping for joy."

Gladys started to laugh at that. Sylvia was right.

Why should she worry about those two? She wouldn't see them again anyway, so what was the big deal?

The big deal was Gladys' life to this point had only amounted to fake friends and ghastly views of her. People were nice enough to her face, but even the best and prettiest flowers talked about her when she wasn't there.

She sighed and went back to the table. She knew she couldn't have everyone love her but knowing that even when she was trying her best to do good some still wouldn't dampen her bright mood of the day .

They continued until she had the curtain pattern and a pillow pattern ready to take back to her current lodgings before she realized the bigger meaning in having the other two teachers gone.

Gladys would have a home. A home she could truly call hers and live in for more than a month at a time. She would have drawers for her clothing and cupboards for dishes. That little tidbit made her downward mood soar to heights she hadn't been to in a good long while.

CHAPTER 34

Mr. Davis came the same day Gladys received another letter from her mother. She already knew, should he ask her to continue, as Gladys wasn't positive, but hopeful, she would sign.

The letter coming beforehand secured it further. It was the usual, sent from her mother complaining about her situation, blaming her for ruining her mother's standing in Deer Lodge, pleading with her to live up to her upbringing and potential.

Essentially, every letter was the same. Her mother would pick different portions to be the focus and seemed to rotate through them, but nothing would change within them. Gladys' choice was always wrong and moving home was the only solution. By this point, she wasn't paying them any mind.

While Gladys didn't let on to Mr. Davis and acted shocked when he broke the news about the other teachers, she didn't have to act when he let her down about the house. He tried to reassure her that she would be moving in, just not at this time. It seemed the house needed a few repairs and she would settle as soon as those were complete.

Gladys hadn't set foot in it before, so she couldn't say what could possibly need repairing, but the blow that came next really sunk her.

Mr. Davis apologized before informing her that she would be staying with the Kilpatricks yet again. Gladys knew exactly why that house signed up for more of her. She wished she didn't, but everyone knew all that woman wanted was a free laborer. With school out, Gladys knew she would be given many more extra tasks than before.

The bright future, that now felt like a carrot dangling in front of her, dimmed with the knowledge of the immediate work ahead. It's not that Gladys shied away from hard work, knowing she was purely being used was the hard part. She would be able to see Sarah frequently again though, and that was the only thing she could hold onto in this situation. Gladys signed the new contract and resolved to move to the Kilpatrick's, who knew for how long.

The next morning was bright and beautiful. A deep blue filled the sky and there wasn't a cloud to be seen. The birds were chirping and fighting to get breakfast. Gladys caught a glimpse of a cottontail bouncing into the brush and saw what must have frightened it, a cat strolling by across the street with his head and tail held high and proud. All the vibrant life around her and she felt miserable.

Gladys dressed and packed for another move, of which she'd lost count. Most moves had lasted exactly a month, but a few were cut a bit shorter and one longer, making it harder to count the exact number anymore.

The drive in Mr. Davis' wagon wasn't long enough, by far. Of course, she knew that she needed to get there and get it over with, but she was also positive no one would find fault in her wanting to delay. Well, maybe Mrs. Kilpatrick of course.

That thought brought a small chuckle as she walked to the door of her last temporary housing. Gladys thought if she kept thinking about it as that it would help to get through it easier.

Gladys immediately discovered that Mrs.

Kilpatrick was not at home. She was relieved as this meant she could settle in before getting her chore list.

Sarah welcomed her and informed her that Momma would be home soon, and she was expecting Gladys to be here and ready to help her when she did arrive. Gladys wasn't surprised but did take a moment to set up her little bed along the wall in the main room, all while telling herself it would be over soon.

Mrs. Kilpatrick didn't waste a minute. She walked in, barking orders for Gladys to take her things and put them away in the kitchen. Apparently, Mrs. Kilpatrick had run an errand to the company store. She also had stopped to pick up the post, as she sat down and was going through the envelopes she'd brought in with her.

Gladys lingered a bit longer in the kitchen than it should have taken her, stealing any moment of free time she could. Hearing her name from the main room meant her life, for the time, was officially over.

"Gladys, welcome back." Mrs. Kilpatrick was quite pleased she was here. Gladys could tell by the giant smile spread across her face.

"I have worked up a regular chore list for you and written it all down. It's quite lengthy, as I know you have ample time on your hands now that school is on break."

Gladys grabbed the list from her and scanned it trying to force her eyes to not show shock. "Thank you." What else was she to say? She didn't want to get on her bad side this soon in her stay.

"Good, then. That will be all. You may start." She dismissed her like a common maid.

"Mrs. Kilpatrick?"

She placed the letter she was reading down on the table and stared expectantly at Gladys. "Yes? Don't just stand there. What is it?"

"I, uh. Well, I wanted. That is, I am reminding you that I do work for Mr. Ulinski once a week. I can set that day, or you can if you would prefer, whatever works best. Now that I'm currently not teaching, my days are very flexible." Gladys started and stopped a couple times before she got it out. Why she let this woman have so much control over her, she didn't know.

"Oh, I remember," she snapped back. "If you can fit it in and still do all that needs done here, fine. Just remember, do not skip meal preparations or you won't be eating." She picked her letter back up indicating the conversation was finished.

"Yes, ma'am. Thank you." Gladys ducked her head

and had to really work to not stomp off. Sarah grabbed her arm and urged her to move quickly away .

They went out back before stopping. "Momma gave me gardening. I hate gardening. I know that you love it, but it's not on your list. I think she did it on purpose."

Gladys took a very unladylike stance and began rubbing the back of her neck. "I'm thinking you are most likely correct in your assumption. She likes to find interesting ways to irritate people."

"I'm sorry she is like this. I wish I knew how to help make her a better person." Sarah plopped onto the grass. If you could call it grass. It was more wisps of green here and there with dirt patches between.

Gladys joined her on the ground. "You can't change someone. Only they can do that. And change is hard." She rolled her eyes and suppressed a chuckle as she thought about the changes she had made. "Just keep your head high and keep dreaming. You are so young. You have a whole life ahead of you away from here."

"Away from Momma at least. Not from here." Sarah grinned. "Paul asked me to marry him. Of course, we are waiting a little while. I want to be married in the fall with all the pretty colors around."

Gladys couldn't fault her for wanting to leave. Mrs. Kilpatrick was like her mother in many ways. She just wished Sarah wouldn't attach herself to someone else so quickly. It could all work out for the best or it could be a disaster.

She had yet to meet this Paul. Really, didn't she do what Sarah was doing? Sure, she wasn't married, but she still had a man in control of her. She left at the first opportunity to do so and, if she had to admit, besides a few very nice friends, it had been a struggle since day one. "I'm very happy for you. I wish you the best."

Sarah hugged her. "Oh, thank you. I was hoping you'd say that."

"What is going on out here?" Mrs. Kilpatrick apparently came to check on them and found them sitting on the ground doing not one item on the list.

Gladys rose, "Sorry, ma'am. Sarah and I were just catching up."

She glared down her nose for a minute before commenting, "Well, all caught up now it looks like. Get to work."

Both girls nodded and parted ways to tackle the first items on their lists.

CHAPTER 35

*W*hen Micha heard Gladys had to stay at the Kilpatrick's again he wanted to spit nails. Then he discovered why, which only infuriated him more. He couldn't fathom how two female teachers could have done damage to the inside of their home. And to have it done all out of anger and pure spitefulness for Gladys getting to stay and them having to leave.

They were mean and hateful people and Micha was glad to see them packing. Although, he never really thought they would stoop that low. Their gossiping and spreading of falsehoods were one thing. This was a whole new level that made him wonder if it was the first time or if other things had occurred of which he was unaware.

He knew asking Mr. Davis what he could do to help get her in faster would just give him more reasons to be teased. Apparently, either he did have it that bad for Miss Wimble, and he was lying to himself or the guys just needed someone to pick on lately, as the kissy faces and batting of eyelashes in his direction by the other miners was getting rather annoying.

Mr. Davis did allow him to help on the repairs, which was why Micha found himself working on the little house on his Monday off. Looking around, he realized the truth behind not having room for Gladys.

The home was tiny. It was two rooms. The main room was large enough to have a stove in the corner that doubled as the cook stove and a table in the center, which doubled as the counter. The other room held two beds and a desk in between. He didn't understand why they didn't accommodate for more teachers when they built the school bigger.

Surveying the damage, he noticed the window had been broken, a few cupboard doors ripped off, and a chair was broken and laying in such a way below the window, he was certain that was how the glass broke. It wasn't that much work. The issue was those who would work on the repairs were doing so in their spare time and that was scarce for a miner.

Micha wanted to give the place a fresh coat of paint, if Mr. Davis had funds for it, to brighten things up for her. She had done so much for him in the short time she had lived in town that he wanted to repay her. He knew he paid her monetarily, but for some reason it didn't feel like enough.

Micha had removed the window casing from the wall when he heard the shriek of the mine whistle. He knew immediately what that meant, as it wasn't ringing at the appropriate time. There was an accident. He dropped everything and ran.

A small crowd had already begun to form, and Micha pushed through them to get to the man cart. He breathed a little easier seeing that the mine itself looked in good shape. He also hadn't felt anything like an explosion. He was just hoping now to hear that no portions of the mine had collapsed.

Micha was trying to enter a cart to descend and find out what was going on when he was stopped by another miner. "Hey, Micha. Can you get the ladies moved out of the way? I don't want them to see what's headed up."

"Sure thing, but what's coming up if I can ask?"

"I don't know everything, but seems a guy wasn't paying attention and was crushed after some big rocks came down in one of our blasts. They got him free and are working to get him above ground now. I hear it's pretty ugly though."

Micha took a breath. He wasn't sure he wanted to see that either. Mining was a dangerous job and paying attention was critical. One second could mean the difference of seeing daylight again or not. He really wanted to know who was injured. He hated that it happened. He had a job to do and needed to do it quickly.

Convincing those ladies it was better to move back so they wouldn't immediately see the damage or who it was, wouldn't be the easiest job. Micha knew they were all worried it was their man and no one would willingly step back, but he put one foot in front of the other and hoped he'd accomplish this minor task in time.

GLADYS AND SARAH were in the backyard pulling blankets from the line when the whistle blared. Gladys was puzzled as she had never heard it at this time of day but glancing at Sarah made her concerned.

Sarah paled and froze, looking as she had just seen a ghost. It was then that Gladys knew something terrible had happened. The conversation with Mary came full force into her mind. Two weeks. Who would it be? Or worse, how many? She dropped to her knees and began praying.

Mrs. Kilpatrick stepped out and saw her daughter frozen where she stood and Gladys on the ground. "What are you doing?" she snapped.

"Momma, the whistle!" Sarah couldn't put more words than that together.

"'Tis, not your concern, girls. Keep working. I didn't feel anything so must not be a cave-in or collapse. I'm sure whatever happened we'll know soon enough, but no sense in wasting our daylight. Get back to work."

She left, and Gladys couldn't comprehend that woman's lack of compassion. She didn't seem phased at all that someone, probably someone she knew, could be injured or worse. Gladys stood and worked, but didn't stop her continual praying.

They were able to get the blankets in and folded up at the foot of the beds, but before they started their next task, a knock sounded on the door.

Sarah answered, and Gladys hovered behind, curious as the whistle made all her nerves stand on end.

"Good day, Miss Sarah. Is your mother home?" Mr. Kemp stood in the doorway looking rather uncomfortable and upset.

Sarah stepped back and called for her mother, who came directly, as she was in the next room.

When she saw Mr. Kemp however, she faltered in her step.

Gladys watched the whole scene unfold. Mr. Kemp spoke quietly to her and grabbed her elbow when he saw she might tip over. He walked her to the table and sat her down.

Sarah had backed up against the wall and was silently crying into her hand. Gladys was fitting all the pieces together and realized the accident involved Mr. Kilpatrick before Mr. Kemp spoke with her.

"Gladys, I would like you to get your things together quickly. You will be staying with us for the time being."

She looked at Sarah who seemed lost in her own world. Gladys nodded and began placing her few items that were out back in her trunk. Mr. Kemp lifted it and the two walked out into the bright sun.

She wished she didn't have to leave Sarah behind, but she had no choice.

Once they were in his wagon she felt free to ask him what had happened. She knew he was holding back some details, but he was truthful about the death.

"What will happen now?" Gladys knew what Mary had said, but thought it couldn't be completely true. It was cruel.

"They now have two weeks to leave or marry. The house will need to be opened up for a new family, should the man we hire to replace him be married."

"But, that's...that's just mean." Gladys fought back her own tears. She wasn't fond of Mrs. Kilpatrick, but she never wished this on anyone. How could anyone be so cruel?

Mr. Kemp sighed. "Gladys, it's not personal. It's just the way mines are run. In order to be profitable, they need to stay working. Working on a smaller crew, even by one, can be more dangerous than not. He knew what he signed on for," he wiped his hand down his face. "We all know."

Gladys turned quiet. She did not like it, but what could she do? Nothing was the answer. No, that wasn't exactly true. She was a teacher. She taught the little boys that would grow up to join the only industry they knew. She could teach them more. Gladys could show them the world, give them desires to do something else. Of course, she knew many would stay and choose this work, but if she could save even one, that would be something.

CHAPTER 36

Summer was rapidly coming to an end and Gladys was busier than ever. She had a school to prepare, to give a tour and introductions to two new teachers, and to settle into her new home.

She was fitting all of that in today but knew all would not be complete by nightfall. Given the situation of her not having a place, Mr. Davis made arrangements that she would have this home for herself for the first year while the other teachers paid their dues by boarding with families. He claimed that it helped them to get to know the community faster. Given her experience, she highly doubted that.

Unfortunately, for those teachers, Mrs. Kilpatrick's home was still available. Cian had dropped school and went to work in the mine allowing the family to stay where they were. Gladys hurt for her to lose her husband, but she didn't want anyone else to be in a position where they had to live with her either. All she could do was warn them ahead of time and speak to Mr. Davis about trying to limit it as much as possible.

Gladys was given the choice of which grade she would teach. She didn't want to change. She loved the youngest kids even if she couldn't dive as deep into topics as she would like to with them.

Mr. Crowley had brought over her trunk to her new house and set it against a wall. Although it needed to be unpacked, for right now it was close enough to the stove in the corner that she could use it to sit on and warm herself during the colder months.

The house was void of anything of comfort, aside from the twin bed and her quilt. Making some curtains and seat cushions for herself was at the top of her list just after she took the ones she made to Micha.

She knew a trip to Tacoma was needed as she was not using any of the selection at the store for herself, but with Sylvia due any moment, Gladys was taking that trip alone.

It wasn't long after that Sadie and Jeffrey came running to her door. They were Gladys' official first guests and she loved it was them.

"Momma let us come and tell you. She's so cute."

Sadie was bouncing up and down.

Jeffrey rolled his eyes at her. "We can't stay, miss. Just wanted to share that Momma delivered Gladys last night."

"Gladys?" She was confused.

"Yes, Momma named her for you. Said we can call her Laly for short so we don't confuse you two." Sadie covered her mouth in the cutest little chuckle she had ever seen.

"She named her for me?"

"Oh silly. We love you. And Momma said you are a good example for me to look up to. Something about you being a good flower."

"Sadie, can we go now? We were told to hurry back." Jeffrey chimed in and then made a pinched face to Gladys, indicating he thought he shouldn't have said it.

"It's all right, you two. Get on home to your Momma. I'm sure she needs your help. Tell her I'm sorry I can't come right away, but I'll be there real soon." She walked them out and waved them on, hollering after they had gone a short distance. "Oh, and tell her thank you. That was very kind of her."

Gladys had a bit more pep in her step while she finished up at home, made a tea tray for three, and walked next door to the school to meet the new teachers.

CHAPTER 37

*S*chool had been in session for a few weeks and Gladys felt she was getting into the swing of things. So far, no animals interrupted the day, all her papers had stayed where she put them, each day when she needed an item it was in the place she had put it, and it was nice.

Gladys didn't know if it was one or both previous teachers pulling all of those stunts or just a student thinking they were being funny, but at this point she really didn't care. Life was going well for her and things were looking up.

Both teachers, Miss Taylor and Miss White, agreed to incorporate lessons about future opportunities. Miss Taylor taught the middle group and was hoping to include visitors from other careers on different days to do a presentation. She would include mine positions as well as logging, as those were the two main industries in this area. She also had a handful of friends from Tacoma that she felt she could get up here for a day, given the short distance of the train.

Given that Miss White's class was mostly girls, she thought giving them time to try teaching was a great idea. Gladys hoped she didn't focus too heavy on just one option, but she did know that she was a new teacher and would learn and adapt as the year went on. Miss White's plans helped Gladys with her little problem from last year that was carrying over to this year. The oldest students would be working on teaching reading to the younger students.

Just after she had started on a math lesson, a knock sounded on her door. Whoever it was didn't wait for her to answer, they opened it and walked in. Gladys had her back turned and didn't see who it was until she pivoted to greet the visitor.

"Good morning, Miss Wimble." Micha removed his hat as he spoke.

"Good morning to you, Mr. Ulinski. Is there something I can help you with? You don't have Lady with you, do you?" She said it only half teasing. To be honest, she had gotten used to having something go awry and was waiting for the next to happen at any time.

Micha chuckled and bobbed his hat up and down pointing it in her direction. "No, no I didn't bring Lady. I actually came to thank you. Our paths haven't crossed in a while and I thought this might be my soonest chance to do it. The little touches you added to my house were just what was needed, and the seat cushions sure make for a more comfortable sit."

Gladys waved it off. "You don't need to thank me for that. I wanted to do something nice and those little touches here and there are what make a house a home."

"I always believed that was from who lived there, but I can see how those touches can help." He winked at her.

Did he just wink at me?

Gladys shook off the thought, explaining it as something in his eye. Then she realized she was blushing. Lord help her! Why was she blushing? She needed him to leave. "Well, it isn't necessary, but you are very welcome. If that's all, I should get back to teaching."

Micha fidgeted a bit. "Well, actually, there was something else I was hoping to say. Or ask, rather."

Gladys looked at him expectantly. She had no idea what Micha could want to ask her.

"Heard about the upcoming wedding." He glanced around at all of the children staring at him. "Maybe we can talk in the hallway?"

"Very well." She instructed her class to continue and reassured that she would be just outside the door and wouldn't be long.

"Well, Gladys, you see, there is a wedding coming up."

"Yes, Sarah's. It's just week after next, I believe. I'm not sure what you would want from me about that, though." Gladys cocked her head to the side and drew her eyebrows in.

"I was hoping you would sit with me. I'd pick you up, but I know you have some strict rules about that. I figure if we are surrounded by most of the town the whole time no one would be able to find fault." He bounced between feet and fiddled with the hat in his hands.

Gladys thought for a moment. Everything was telling her to say no. She wanted to teach, not marry. Oh, but he was so kind to her and they were friends, after all. Maybe if she presented it in a friendly way he would understand, but she wouldn't hurt him with a no. "I would love to sit with you. I don't have many friends yet. Although, several people are beginning to open up to me, now. Having a closer friend to sit with would be very nice." She hoped she used the word friend enough to get the message across. His excited smile left her in doubt.

"Uh, all right, then. I guess if I don't see you before, I'll see you at the wedding. I'll have a chair saved for you." He locked eyes with her a bit longer than she was comfortable with.

She broke the gaze and he took that as a sign to leave. Gladys stood with her hand on the doorknob, not sure how she felt. She did like Micha, as a friend. Could it become more? She really wasn't sure.

Talking all this over with Sylvia was most needed. Gladys usually was able to straighten things out with her and she needed to go see the new darling. She settled her plan and pushed the thoughts aside as best she could to finish this day.

CHAPTER 38

Sitting in a rocking chair holding her namesake, Gladys stared into the blue eyes that glistened looking back at her. She was working to breathe through her mouth. Gladys didn't want to tell Sylvia that her house smelled, but she hoped the smell left soon. She knew Mr. Crowley wouldn't say anything. He might step in and work to get rid of it himself, but he wouldn't complain to Sylvia.

When she arrived, Laly had been wailing. Sylvia seemed beside herself in worry. As soon as Gladys took her she calmed down.

"You have a way with babies." Sylvia sat down and rubbed her shoulder. She looked tired, with heavy eyes.

Gladys patted Laly's back. "I've never been around babies much. I don't know what I did, but it worked."

"I don't know, either. Babies are a mystery sometimes. Whatever it was, though, please, keep it up."

Gladys chuckled. "I'll try, but I'm not promising anything."

She paused, unsure if she should ask her how she was fairing, but thought honesty was best.

"Sylvia, you look tired. How are you doing?"

Sylvia chuckled now. "Yes, I'm tired. The joys of having a newborn. Laly is a bit fussier than my first two. I'm not sure what the problem is, but we are doing the best we can. And Sadie, bless her heart, wants to be the biggest helper she can, which means she is constantly under foot and in the way."

"Sadie is a wonderful girl and is a big help at school."

Sylvia got up and got busy. "I hope you don't mind, but since she has decided that now, when I have extra hands here, is the perfect time to sleep, I'm going to take advantage of that and get some things done around here."

Gladys smiled and snuggled in a bit more with the baby. "I don't mind at all. She is so soft and warm."

Laughing, Sylvia shot back. "Soft and warm now. She becomes a furnace at times. Please, though, tell me something other than babies. I want to talk about something else. I've been cooped up in here day in and day out with Laly." She wiped down the table. "I know... How did Micha like his new decorations?"

It was interesting that Sylvia mentioned Micha. Gladys originally came to discuss her situation with him but wasn't sure how to approach the subject. It seemed Sylvia helped her once again. "I think he liked them. He came by the other day to thank me for it."

"He came by your house or the school?"

"He stopped by the school. We spoke in the hall-way. Actually, our conversation was what brought me here today."

"Oh?" Sylvia paused with the rag midair. Now, Gladys had her full attention.

If Gladys could get up and pace, she would.

Waking Laly was not an option. "Yes, he thanked me and then asked me to go to Sarah's wedding with him."

"He did what? What did you say?"

Gladys rolled her head a bit. "Well, I was worried at first. I can't be alone with a man. He can't pick me up or drop me off. It seemed he already knew that and planned for that. He said he would meet me there and we could sit together. I did eventually say yes, but I don't know if I should."

"What do you mean if you should? Of course, you should."

"Really?" Gladys didn't want to encourage him, but she didn't want to hurt him either.

Sylvia came and sat back down by her. "Yes, you should. He's a great guy and I think both of you would be good together."

"Oh!" Gladys wasn't sure what to say now. She didn't want to hurt Sylvia. It seemed she really wanted them together. "I guess I am not sure if I ever want to be married."

Sylvia pushed her lips together watching her. "I see. I just assumed you'd eventually want to settle down and have children of your own someday." She looked between Gladys and Laly.

Gladys thought a bit. Did she ever want her own children? Her class seemed to fill that desire for now, but Gladys wasn't sure if it would sustain or dwindle as the years went on.

If she did want children, she knew that would need to happen soon. But she loved teaching and having one meant giving up the other. "Oh, I don't know. I love my job. I love the kids. I can't have both."

"Why don't you just go and sit with him. Get to know him more. I know you do, somewhat, know him. Actually, you know more than some, with cleaning up after him." She chuckled. "You know the dirty side of marriage, but not the best part. If you pick well, you get to be married to your best friend."

"And if I don't?"

"Well, let's just hope you do, if you do."

"My parents don't have the best relationship. I honestly don't know if my love of teaching and aversion to marriage are directly related to watching them as I grew up or not. I haven't had time to really think about it. Just learning how to be a friend and find my place has taken up most of my time."

"I understand. You have made big changes in a short time. Don't rush anything with Micha, but I think you need to give him a chance for the both of you."

Gladys thanked her and gently passed Laly to her. Luckily, she stayed asleep. At least briefly. Gladys heard the first of her cries when she shut the front door. She took a deep breath of fresh air and set a slow pace walking home, thinking about everything Sylvia had said.

She couldn't answer if she wanted to teach because she loved it or if it was to prevent getting married. Listening to her parents argue off and on was a big reason why she never wanted that life. It took living with other families to know that not all were that way. She had never seen any other married couple out right fight in front of her in the past, but her parents didn't fight with each other in front of anyone else either. She just assumed behind closed doors they were much of the same.

In the end, she decided Sylvia was right. She needed to give Micha a chance...not only for him, but for herself, too. She had to test the waters before she could know how she really felt. She just hoped no one ended up with a broken heart in the process.

CHAPTER 39

The wedding was held in Saint Aloysius Parish, which sat just a few blocks away, on a crisp and cold early October morning. The weather was foggy, but the rains held off, making travel fair. The Crowley's drove Gladys so she wouldn't have to walk, despite the dry conditions, and she was grateful she wouldn't be freezing cold by the time she arrived.

It was a simple affair. There were no flowers decorating the pews or sanctuary. The large windows let in plenty of light, making the room feel cheery despite the dreary day. It seemed the whole town came out to celebrate with Sarah and Paul, as the rows were mostly filled and Gladys was warmed to see the support. Having Mrs. Kilpatrick as your mother might make everyone run for the hills. Either they clearly liked Sarah or they needed some excitement and something to do. I'm sure Sarah wouldn't mind either reason.

She knew why Sarah wanted to leave. She was already keeping house and taking care of her younger brothers as it was. Gladys was certain that early married life would, most likely, be like a vacation for her. She just hoped that as the newness wore off she would still like her decision.

Gladys herself, could ask the same question of her own choice. Her teaching was still new. She was the newcomer in the town, despite having two newer teachers. It would take a while to settle in and become fully accepted here. Would she then like her choice or would something else pull her in a different direction?

Gladys looked over at Micha, who was sitting to her left, and smiled at him. She supposed she really did need to keep all options open until she knew for certain what her future should be. She just hoped she didn't lead him on in the process. Crushing someone else was not something she wanted to do willingly. She mentally shook her thoughts away and turned her attention to the front of the church.

Sarah was dressed in her best Sunday dress.

Gladys only knew this because she knew her and her clothes. It was made from the standard materials found in the company store. The best that could be said was that it fit properly, and she did her best to make it as festive as possible by carrying a bunch of vibrantly colored leaves. They were still perky, so Gladys assumed she had someone gather them right before the wedding started.

She could see why Sarah wanted the fall colors for her wedding. The yellows, oranges, and reds looked beautiful against her navy dress.

After the ceremony, everyone filed outside to congratulate the happy couple. During the summer months, she was sure there would have been food or at least coffee, but since there wasn't a gathering place indoors, nothing was prepared. She and Micha had yet to really talk. It would have been rude to speak during the wedding and now they were just awkwardly standing about with everyone milling around.

"Gladys, we will be leaving in a few minutes. I don't want Laly out in this cold weather too long." Mr. Crowley spoke to her and nodded to Micha.

"Do you mind if I walk her home, sir?" Micha wasn't ready to part and was grasping for ideas to continue.

Mr. Crowley looked between them. "Well, technically you shouldn't be alone. Walking on the road in broad daylight would, most likely be fine, except now that you two were seen by the town sitting together, tongues will already be wagging. I'm not sure if you want to add fuel to their fire this soon. That is up to you, of course. I won't stand in your way ."

"Oh my! I certainly don't want people spreading anything about me. I had that enough already. With those two teachers gone, I'm finally feeling accepted and people are speaking to me instead of staring. I'm sorry, Micha, but maybe we could see each other again in another way, one that wouldn't cause rumors to fly."

Micha sighed, "Whatever you feel is best."

"Why don't we set up a supper at our house where you two can get to know each other a bit more?" Mr. Crowley's face held a tinge of smugness.

"That sounds perfect! Micha does that work for you?" Gladys looked up at him, hopeful.

"I'm sure that would be fine. Just let me know when and I'll show up hungry."

"Good. I'll talk with my missus and let you both know when to come. Gladys, come on, dear. We really do need to get going."

Gladys looked between the two. She felt awful for having to leave Micha now. She thought he was expecting more from today. She didn't know what to expect herself, but a little conversing was probable.

"It was nice to sit with you today. I look forward to the supper."

"Yes, thank you for joining me. Until next time." Micha turned and left awkwardly. It seemed neither of them knew what to do or how to move forward with this, whatever this was.

"Come along, now. We'll be home and getting warm in no time, but we must leave now."

Gladys took Mr. Crowley's offered arm and they headed for the wagon that was already waiting with his little family loaded. Before they got within ear shot, she leaned in a bit and spoke to him quickly.

"I'm not sure how to ask this, but I don't have time to work at forming it delicately. Is the house, or will the house be smell-free by the supper you suggested?"

Mr. Crowley wrinkled his forehead in confusion at her.

"See, I was there the other day and it smelled of, well, dirtiness that can only come from humans."

Mr. Crowley began to chuckle. "Well, I can't guarantee the smell from waste will not make itself known then, as babies tend to do that frequently. I will make sure Sadie takes care of the soiled linens before either of you arrive."

Mr. Crowley wailed in laughter the rest of the way to the wagon causing Sylvia to chuckle and ask what he was laughing about. To Gladys' horror he told her. Instead of being offended or angry with her, she thought it was the funniest thing in the world. The whole wagon was a barrel of laughs all the way home. Gladys was mortified, despite Sylvia apologizing multiple times to her through her chortles. Gladys didn't really see what was that funny with it. It stunk.

CHAPTER 40

Gladys found herself on the next Friday night sitting around the Crowley table. She wasn't feeling well, but thought it was just nerves. Micha sat to her right and Sadie and Jeffrey were across from them. She had calmed considerably regarding the previous event. In the past, if anyone laughed at her, it would be immediate revenge. Whatever could hurt them the worst the quickest would be the best route. Now she realized they didn't laugh at her in a mean way. It was funny, and after some time passed, she saw some of the humor.

Gladys took a while preparing for tonight, not sure what to wear. Most of the pretty dresses her mother sent were too bright or showy for her career choice. With a couple of alterations on some she was able to use them for special occasions. The darker colored ones worked for that. There was nothing she could do with the bold colors of the rest.

She slipped into the maroon colored one that was belted at the waist and held a wide collar that made a vee in the front. Gladys added one of her frilly blouses under to increase the neckline well above where it drew the eyes before. This dress was also the easiest to alter to make it appropriate enough for a teacher after hours.

"So, Micha, tell us about your family." Sylvia tried for small talk to get the conversation flowing.

Micha wiped his mouth with his napkin. He had been thoroughly enjoying Sylvia's cooking, but Gladys didn't fault him for his eagerness to dig in. She knew he didn't always have a hot cooked meal to come home to. He proceeded to tell her about his parents and siblings back home. From there he dove into a full history of his home country.

By the time he finished, Gladys had finished what she could eat of her supper, which wasn't much given her upset stomach. She had learned much about Micha. He was very loyal to his family and his country. She was surprised to hear that he sent wages home in addition to what he paid her.

Gladys thought that was noble of him. She wondered if he was ready to settle down. Could he take care of a wife and eventually a family with what was left after his obligations were met?

Of course, he wouldn't be paying her to clean for him if she lived there as his wife. That would free up some, but not much, and Gladys would lose her income. Somehow, she felt she wasn't supposed to be thinking about the logistics of the marriage, but whether she wanted to marry in the first place. She pulled herself back into the conversation at the perfect time as Micha was asking her about her family .

Gladys gave him the short version. She didn't want to scare him off too soon. She liked their friend- ship, after all. She noticed Sylvia was smirking at her. Apparently, she knew her game.

She moved into talk about where she came from. She could elaborate there. Deer Lodge was a wonderful town now that she appreciated it from a new perspective. The people were close-knit and worked together to pull through tough times when needed.

After dinner Micha took his leave, and Gladys walked him to the door. Sylvia put the kids on cleanup so they would stay in the opposite side of the house. Micha stood just outside, and Gladys used the door to block those inside from seeing much.

"This was great. Thanks for this." Micha had his hands in his pockets and she was sure he would have been fidgeting if he didn't.

"Thank you, but I didn't plan this. This was all Mr. Crowley."

"So, is there another time? Something else we can do?"

Gladys paused, thinking, "I'm not really sure what we can do. Maybe you should ask Mr. Davis for suggestions? I don't want to break my contract." She hoped she didn't sound as though she didn't want to see him again. She had a nice time, but she didn't know yet how she felt about him. He was a good guy and a hard worker. And he'd been good around kids and his dog. He also would not be approved by her mother. In other words, he had all the makings of a perfect pick, should she be looking. That was the crux of the problem. Should she be looking?

She said goodbye and he quickly put a kiss to her cheek, which stunned her frozen. She had never been kissed before by anyone except her father. Even her own mother didn't see the need. She didn't know what to make of that. By the time she was able to move again, he had gone. She spun back in the house and shut the door. Sylvia was pretending to be busy but came quickly after the click of the door.

"Well? Oh, come here, tell me everything. What do you think? Now I know you already know him, but did you see him any differently tonight?"

Gladys sat but didn't really know what to say. "I'm not sure."

"What do you mean you're not sure? Did you have any funny stomach feelings or a calm feeling of peace?"

Gladys wasn't sure what Sylvia was talking about. "Well, I did have an upset stomach when I got here. I thought it was getting worse, but when I started talking it seemed to calm down. I don't know how I feel about him. Tonight just felt awkward."

"It's supposed to be awkward," Sylvia huffed like she was put out.

"I'm sorry. You went to all this trouble and I can't even answer a question appropriately."

Sylvia waved the apology away. "No worries. It's been so long since I have been in this situation, I seem to have forgotten how hard it can be."

Gladys felt a little better and wanted to offer Sylvia something. "He did kiss me at the door."

"He what? Oh, this is good news. And how did you feel about that?"

Gladys thought a bit, rolling the scene back in her head. "It startled me. I've never been kissed before."

"No sparks flew?" She leaned closer in anticipation and was subtly rocking.

This was a side of Sylvia she had never seen before. She was always the motherly sort, offering advice but never forcing Gladys to where she hoped she would go. Now she was acting like they were both silly school girls. Gladys wasn't sure what to think of that. She was really considering if she should be concerned. A new baby was hard work and Sylvia had been cooped up for weeks with only church days out. Gladys decided that Sylvia should be put on watch and she needed to come around more frequently .

"No sparks flew. I was frozen. I couldn't think for a minute. When I finally came around, he was gone."

Sylvia looked in deep thought. She waved it all off and stood. "No worries. It's just the first night and the first kiss. Time will tell. You'll see."

Gladys watched her change back into normal Sylvia directing her kids to what still needed doing to clean up and taking care of Laly. She didn't want to talk to Mr. Crowley about her concern for Sylvia, but she thought she needed to. She couldn't very well say anything in front of Sylvia, though, so she thought she would wait until he took her home. Her behavior wasn't odd for some ladies, but it was odd for her. Gladys decided maybe the best thing to do in the meantime was pitch in and help with whatever needed to be done.

MICHA WAS on cloud nine the whole way home. He wasn't sure before he went if he should try to kiss her good night, but in the moment, it felt right. When he first met Gladys, he thought her to be a stuck-up snobbish girl. She seemed too focused on herself to care for others. Through the months he'd noticed a change.

It started with little things that she did for him at his house that went above and beyond her job duties. She would make sure he had a decent meal or, at the very least, a warm fire to cook it on. She took care of Lady like her own and most recently she added a hominess he didn't know he was missing until he had it. Micha missed his family and his country, but Gladys gave him a sense of home right here.

Finding someone to spend your life with who cared as much about you as they did themselves was a rare treat. Those were the keepers. Micha wanted to grab onto that and never let go.

He thought briefly about stopping by Mr. Davis' home before his. He wanted to figure out how to see her again and didn't want to wait. The hour was late and he didn't want to interrupt their family time together. Micha decided waiting until morning would be best.

CHAPTER 41

Gladys was able to express her concerns for Sylvia on the drive to her home. Mr. Crowley, however, didn't seem to see a problem.

If he didn't think there was an issue, Gladys was wondering if perhaps then the nerves from that night played into her overthinking and creating something that wasn't really there.

That excuse didn't sit well with her. The personality change was what concerned her. She was sure something was off. In the months past, Gladys had never seen Sylvia act anything but the perfect mother.

Because she was not settled, despite her talk with Mr. Crowley, she found herself using her weekend to help Sylvia with whatever needed to be done. She was watching her, but nothing seemed amiss thus far.

Gladys was working on the laundry and Sadie was helping. Jeffrey had run off with a group of boys, probably playing in some mud puddle, making more laundry.

She decided to take this time to talk with Sadie, but Sadie seemed to be of no help. Given her young age, Gladys should have known better, but trying didn't hurt anything.

Gladys didn't want to talk about it with Sylvia, but she didn't know how else to calm her worry. She knew if she didn't say anything, the concern would only deepen. She also knew not to start the conversation with Sadie present, so she took the liberty to send her off to play with some friends.

"Sylvia, could I speak with you a moment?"

Bouncing Laly and patting her back, Sylvia nodded. Gladys wished they could sit to talk, but Laly most likely wouldn't cooperate for that. She tried to form what she was going to say as delicately as possible.

"I was hoping to talk about last evening."

This perked Sylvia up some.

"You seemed different that night. I was just

wondering if you were feeling well." Gladys was fidgeting with her apron.

"Different?" Sylvia pondered a bit. "I felt fine. I'm not sure what you mean."

"Well, normally you are more reserved. Usually less likely to excite and seem to take everything in before you form an opinion."

Sylvia chuckled, "You mean after Micha left, right?"

"Yes."

"Oh Gladys, I was just being your sister."

Gladys did not understand what she meant by that at all.

"I know with my three kids and husband I seem all grown up and just the mom, but I'm not that much older than you. I do like a good, juicy conversation from time to time. Besides, you already have a mother and I thought in this moment you could use a sister."

"But you've acted more of a mother all along."

"Well, that's because when you first moved here and for a while that's what you needed. And sometimes you might still need more of a mother figure as you weave through life. I know that you haven't had the best relationship with your mother and she hasn't given you the best advice. I thought you could use some guidance. You've also never had a sister or friend close enough to be one. This situation warranted that role. That one's more fun, too." Sylvia winked.

"Oh, but I just thought maybe with all the stress of having a new one, and I know she hasn't been the easiest at times, maybe you were in need of a break."

"Well, a break I could use, but no. You haven't seen every side to me yet. Honey, there's more where that came from." Sylvia cocked her head while she said it.

Gladys covered her mouth to laugh and relaxed a bit. Sylvia was right in that she had only been here a bit over a year. She couldn't know enough about Sylvia to know this wasn't normal behavior. As they continued their conversation the door blew open and Sadie burst in with Micha in toe.

"Momma, look who I found walking our way." Sadie was pulling him in by the arm and Micha had a sheepish look on his face.

"So sorry for the disturbance, but since I'm here I was hoping to speak with Gladys."

Sylvia covered a giggle with a cough. "Oh, excuse me. I do believe I need some water and it's well past time for me to start on supper. Sadie come with me, please."

Gladys stood, unsure of what to do. Sylvia and Sadie left the room and Micha seemed to fill it up. She still wasn't sure how she felt about him. Since the previous night she had thought long and hard about what a life with Micha might look like. She just couldn't shake the faces of her students out of her mind no matter how hard she tried. Those were her children and she didn't think she could give them up for him. At least not yet.

Gladys thought maybe with time he would become more of an importance to her. She barely knew him so that made sense. Perhaps getting to know him more would change everything.

"Hello, Gladys. I stopped by your house, but obviously you weren't there. This was the next place I knew to look."

"Well, you found me. What did you want to talk about?" Gladys anchored her hands onto her skirt, so she didn't fidget with them.

Micha looked around a bit nervously. "Uh, here, can we sit?" He gestured towards the chairs at by the fire.

"Oh, yes, of course, I guess." This wasn't her home. Gladys felt a bit awkward acting as hostess. Both awkwardly sat.

Silence ensued. Neither one knew what to say

next. They both sat looking at each other waiting for the other one to speak.

"I enjoyed last night," they both began in unison and then laughed.

"I had a chance to speak with Mr. Davis today. He asked if we would like to join him and Mrs. Davis for a late afternoon picnic next week, weather permitting of course."

"Do you think it will be warm enough? It's getting so cold. I'm not sure I'm ready yet for the winter."

"As long as the rain holds off and the fog lifts, it should be decent enough. I'm sure Mrs. Davis will pack hot foods and drinks."

"Oh, I do have a large school project all three of us teachers are working on. I'm not sure I'll have time." Gladys wasn't sure if she wanted to go.

"Does Mr. Davis know about the project? If not, maybe you could use the time to share. I'm sure, being the head of the school, he would find that fascinating."

Would Micha find it fascinating? Gladys knew Mr. Davis would love to know. He cared about his position and about the students. Somehow Gladys felt she should know how Micha felt. She should ask him.

Knowing that was important to her if they were going to become serious, but she wouldn't ask yet. She felt she didn't know him well enough to start asking questions like that. She didn't want Micha to think she liked him beyond a friend before she knew if she did.

"I'll see what I can do. I can't promise you. It depends on how the preparations go. I know Mr. Davis would not be happy knowing that I put a social invitation before my students."

"Is there something I can do to help you?" Gladys grinned. "I'm sorry, but no."

Micha shrunk in his seat. "I'll come find you next week to see if you are free."

Gladys nodded with a smile on her face, but she felt the hurt she could see on his face. "That sounds just fine."

Awkward silence followed again before Micha stood to leave. Sylvia walked back in at that moment. "Are you taking off so soon?"

"Yes, ma'am. I need to be on my way. Thank you for letting me speak with Gladys. Take care."

Sylvia watched him leave before she asked Gladys what that was all about.

"You what?"

"I told him maybe. I don't know if I can go."

Gladys rose from her chair, "Why is everyone so intent on speeding things up around here anyway?"

Sylvia snapped her head. "Speeding things up? What do you mean?"

Gladys started her pacing. "Well, Sarah and Paul for one. They are just babies and now hitched with no time to really get to know each other. Now Micha. We just saw each other yesterday. Now he wants to see me again."

"Oh, I see. Gladys come sit." The ladies settled into the chairs Gladys and Micha had just left. "Gladys dear, you live in a mining town. We move fast. We must. Tomorrow is never a guarantee. Anything can happen. Now that is true for everyone, but it seems to ring truer in towns like ours. I'm not much older than you are, but I've seen it happen to many of our people. Pray to God every morning it won't be me."

Gladys hadn't thought about it that way. Her thoughts turned to Mrs. Kilpatrick. She'd had a rough life and had been dealt hard blows too many times. It hardened her.

Gladys felt horrible for that. It wasn't right how Mrs. Kilpatrick treated others, but one could understand where the bitterness came from at least. "I'm sorry. I never thought about that."

"Well, of course not. You are new to this way of life. Besides, it's not as if you two just started knowing each other. You've known him and have been learning little bits here and there for over a year now."

Gladys chewed her lip. "Yes. I suppose so."

"All right, then. Cut him some slack. Go on the picnic." Sylvia headed back to the kitchen to presumably work on supper and left Gladys alone.

People here expected quick decisions and that meant Micha would also. She knew she couldn't give him that. He was a friend. She didn't feel anything more for him yet and didn't think she could speed things up to try to find it.

She pushed herself up and made for home without saying good bye. Sylvia knew she had much on her mind and Gladys didn't think it would bother her. She dearly hoped so anyway.

CHAPTER 42

Micha had started work on carving a ring for Gladys. They had met a few more times, all supervised, and he was now sure.

What he didn't know was how she felt about it.

In many ways Gladys shared qualities with his own mother: she was strong and determined, but soft and considerate. She would make the perfect wife for him and mother of their children.

He decided he would ask her to marry him at Christmas. That was only a month away and he thought that would give plenty of time for her to know if she didn't yet.

The only hesitation he had was his difficulty with reading. He hoped that wouldn't make her shy away from him. Even though he had a good grasp of her character, he still wasn't sure on this one issue. He wanted to think that she would see his abilities to be a good provider and not focus on what he couldn't do. Micha tossed around whether he should tell her before he asked her or wait until after. Of course, just not saying anything and letting her figure it out on her own was an option. He didn't know which way was the right way but he did have some time to think it over for a bit.

On the job front, Micha was succeeding at the electrical position. He had learned enough that he was now working solo on every shift. He felt proud of his accomplishments. With the extra pay he was able to send more back home and felt he could provide nicely for a family.

Everything was lining up for him. For the longest time he had doubted if coming to America was the best choice, but now he knew it was, without doubt. This opportunity or anything close to it would have never been possible back home.

In fact, in his last letter, he asked if anyone else wanted to come. He saved up and would pay for their ship over. If Gladys said yes and he did marry that would cut into his extra finances. He knew this, but he also knew that his parents would be happy despite the dip in money sent.

"Hey, Micha!" A shout came from behind him. "You all right up here?"

Micha turned. "Oh, hey, Jakub. How are you doing?"

"I'm all right, but it seems we have an issue that needs your attention."

"I'll get right on that. Thanks."

Jakub chuckled and shook his head. "No problem. Just try to keep your head on straight, at least while you're here working. I want to remain in the land of the living and that means we all need to stay focused."

Micha rubbed the back of his neck. "I understand that. Thanks again." Christmas couldn't come soon enough this year. He knew he'd be stewing over this until he had her answer.

STARING AT HER STUDENTS, Gladys still wasn't sure she could give up all this. She stood behind her desk and looked at the group, all with their noses in books. They filled her heart the way no one else had before. Most of them had a need to learn. They ate it up and she relished that. She used this quiet time to think over Micha and their times together.

She had met with Micha a handful of times. She thought she should know if something was there or not by now and so did Sylvia. The awkwardness that was present every time they were together lessened with each time and the friendship seemed to grow deeper, too.

That's all she felt. Micha was a friend and a good one at that. Gladys was feeling very comfortable with him. But she wanted sparks. She wanted obvious. Instead of the deep devotion and longing looks from Micha, all she saw was a need he wanted to fill. He looked at her like she would suit his purpose.

She had talked it all over with Sylvia a few times now. Sylvia just kept saying that the best relationships could come from a friendship and to keep going. She also suggested that Gladys think back on all their times together to see if she missed something that would change her view. So now, as she was supposed to be teaching, she was doing just that. Starting with their first meeting from right here in this very room.

Gladys and Micha had been officially meeting regularly now for over a month. It had been about four months, being now November, since the work on her little home was started.

Gladys discovered he spent most of his free time fixing it up and she was thankful for that. Even that didn't draw her closer to him, though. There was something there that didn't fit. They didn't fit. She wasn't sure why, but she knew whatever it was, it prevented her from moving beyond a friend or brother feeling.

When she thought back on last Christmas, she thought she had her an 'ah moment'. Something was off then. She knew it but couldn't put her finger on it. Gladys supposed that was the hold-up with her. Maybe if she could pinpoint exactly what was off she could move on from it.

Without knowing the cause she didn't know if it was possible. She felt like he was hiding something from her, which didn't fit with what she knew Micha to be. If he was hiding something it must be big, or at least he thought it was.

"Miss Wimble?" A little boy sitting towards the back of the room was standing looking directly at her.

"Ivan, you know you are supposed to raise your hand and wait to be called on."

"Yes, Miss, but I did that, for quite a while, and you haven't noticed."

Gladys looked shocked. Had she really been that lost in thought that she wasn't paying attention to her pupils? "I'm sorry. What is it you need?"

"I can't read this word, Miss. I was hoping you could help me."

Can't read. That's it! It all fit. Not writing down the song himself, singing different lyrics than what was written on the page he provided. Struggling at work until he memorized the diagram. It all fell into place. Of course, she suspected that, or something related to that, but now it all seemed to click.

"Thank you, Ivan. I think you gave me the answer I was searching for."

His eyebrows rose. "I did? Can you still help me with my reading?"

Gladys laughed, "Yes, of course I can." She walked back to him and sounded out the word, adventure, with him. Gladys left him to keep working as she walked back to her desk to contemplate her new revelation.

Micha fit as a student. He could use her help as a teacher. That must be why she couldn't move past a friendship into a romantic relationship with him. Now, what to do with that information?

Micha obviously didn't want her to know, but did he really think he could keep something like that from her? Was starting a marriage with a lie like that a good thing? She didn't think so.

Maybe after she had taught him to read they could move into a more serious relationship. She knew now that wasn't possible with the current situation. She had thought if she could figure out what the hiccup was, she could move past it, but now she knew that was impossible. If her revelation was correct, she would think of him as someone to teach until that job was finished. She had no idea how to approach him about this subject. Given the fact that he had kept it from her he would probably be mortified to know she figured it out. She had no idea how to move from here.

CHAPTER 43

*A*nother work day started for Micha. With the hope of Gladys as his future and a large wonderful meal ahead, he was joyful. Thanksgiving was right around the corner, being set the prior month by President Wilson on the 25th of this year, the last Thursday of November as usual. They would all have a rare Thursday off, and his mouth was already watering, knowing he would attend the multifamily celebration where some of the best cooks in town pulled together to make the feast.

No more holiday nights being spent with the other single men for him. The whole town knew of him and Gladys and many were sure a wedding was soon to be announced, securing them as one of the families of the community. He beamed.

A fuse had blown, causing the hoist not to operate. Micha had been working on it for a while, to no avail. Since it was taking a while, a decision was made to send the bulk of the crew home until it was fixed. Most of the miners sent home didn't want to go but had no choice. It meant no pay for the day. Since Micha handled the electrical operations, he stayed and was thankful for it. Only around 50 men were allowed to keep working as best they could while he tried repairing the problem.

Micha went about his work, whistling all the while until the short toot sounded for lunch. Given the job he was required to do meant he would go without lunch until the hoist was fixed. He knew the expectation without asking, despite the thought of sitting outside enjoying lunch in the pleasant November day.

Most days were gloomy, but today was rare. He savored any time he could be above ground. Many of the men would join him as they, too, loved the feel of the sun on their faces. Today would be a missed opportunity for that, as getting the mine up and running again was his only focus.

By early afternoon the mine was still down. Micha was doing everything he knew but was at a loss for how to fix it. A few men came at various times to offer help, but nothing was working. He didn't want to disappoint or upset anyone as he started having doubts on his ability.

THE DAY WAS LOVELY. Gladys couldn't remember the last time they had such a beautiful day. This fall was wet, but today was dry and beautiful. Earlier, Gladys had joined the students outside for lunch. It was such a pleasant day; she didn't want to miss it.

The children loved it since she didn't do this often. Being outside meant they were able to see many men wandering through town. Gladys thought that was odd, but no one seemed worried, so she didn't either.

After lunch they filed back into the classroom to work on their math lesson. They were working on carrying, which was difficult for all her students, but especially for the youngest who were still grasping the concept of basic addition and subtraction.

It was a stressful lesson, to say the least, but one that must be taught. Everyone was feeling the effects of a full stomach and struggling with the lesson. They were all sleepy. Gladys thought they needed a bit of a rest. They didn't do it daily, but these younger kids benefited from resting now and then. She let them lay their heads down on their desks for a bit while she sat at her desk and worked on other things.

It wasn't much longer when all of the sudden a boom ricocheted through the room and the whole school shook. The children flew up and some screamed, while others began to cry. Gladys worked to calm them, saying she thought they had a little earthquake. The little ones seemed to calm down with that, although even knowing the cause was still scary. Some of the older boys were insisting it was a mine issue, though. She couldn't shake them.

It seemed forever but it was only minutes when the school was stormed by men racing for the closet. The one she was told not to go into. The one that held the rescue equipment. That was when she knew. That was when a panic began to take hold and she, with the students in tow, ran up the hill.

Those joining her group were all in the same state of panic. Everyone was pushing and shoving to climb up the trail. Men, women, and children were all in various stages of concern and worry. It wasn't until she got to the top that she noticed the massive black cloud pouring out of the main entry shaft. It was at that moment she dropped to her knees and prayed like she'd never done before.

CHAPTER 44

Gladys remained on her knees while cries and shouts erupted around her. People were frantically running in circles.

Everyone wanted to know who was down there. Some women and children were ecstatic to meet their husbands and fathers amongst the growing crowd. She didn't know how long she remained there until someone tapped her on her shoulder.

"Sylvia! I don't, I can't."

"It's all right. I understand." Sylvia helped Gladys up and wrapped her in a tight hug.

"Mr. Crowley?"

"He's helping with the other men."

Gladys pulled back, "So he wasn't down there?" Sylvia, with tears in her eyes, shook her head.

"There was a malfunction and most of the men were sent home early. Many of them went to Georgetown instead of going home, which is why families are just now meeting up and learning they are all right. Others went straight home."

"Mr. Crowley. Did he come home?"

Sylvia nodded. They held each other for minutes, hours, neither knew for certain.

"What now?"

Taking a deep breath, she shrugged. "A search is already underway. They will work to pull out the survivors before bringing out the deceased. This is all provided they can get to them. If it's a full cave-in people could be buried hundreds of feet deep."

Gladys was in shock. Her mind was struggling to comprehend. "And what after?"

Sylvia was quiet. Too quiet. "Sylvia? What after?"

"They're out. Depending on the damage, we might all be."

Gladys staggered backwards. All? Her too? What would she do? Where would she go? Thoughts circled and circled in her head.

"Gladys. Gladys. Gladys!" Sylvia yelled to snap her back to attention. "Let's gather any of the women folk we can find that know their husbands are safe. Those rescuing will need food. We should pull together to provide it. You circle around that way and I'll go this way. We'll meet in the middle and then head to my house to form a plan. Tell everyone, my house."

Gladys ran and was working quickly. She only approached those who didn't look distraught and she asked about their family first. All the men were now close to the mine, figuring out what to do.

The women were scattered in small groups all around. Gladys could hear shouts of men organizing. Some would get word out to the nearest towns to bring in more help. The others would start working on a side entry shaft to see if that point was safe to enter since the main shaft was billowing thick black smoke that seemed to reach the heavens.

"Mrs. Davis, Mrs. Kemp?"

They blankly stared at her. "Your husbands are prominent members. Surely they were sent home today. It'd be the newer hires and green men left to work."

Mrs. Kemp shook her head no.

Gladys' eyes blurred from tears and her chin quivered.

"Mr. Kemp's gonna be just fine. You'll see. He's in that cement box of his. They just need to get to him is all. His will be done. We have to remember that."

Mary and Gladys both looked at Mrs. Davis apologetically knowing Mr. Davis did not have a safe box in which to stay protected.

"Right. Okay. I'll keep praying." She moved on, not knowing what else to say.

When they finally met up at the Crowley residence the group was small in comparison to the size of the town. Some women who were still up at the mine could have come but chose to not leave friends who were waiting for news. It was difficult to pull away those who did come, but knowing they could do something that would help in some way encouraged them. After taking a quick inventory of what everyone was stocked up with, they divided into small groups to work in various houses pulling it all together.

As they worked on the food, they could see men running through the streets. Sylvia told her they most likely were from Black Diamond, as that was the closest mine. She assumed those from other mining towns would be on their way as well. All the small mining towns around were rivals on the baseball field, but at the end of the day, they were brothers by trade and would do anything for a fellow miner.

They worked silently for a long while. Gladys

had lots of questions, but Sylvia didn't seem to want to talk. She decided to test the waters a little as her worry was getting the better of her.

"Have you ever seen anything like this before?" Gladys was still trying to grasp the situation.

Pounding dough with a fist that was turning red from hitting it too hard she simply said "No."

Gladys hadn't yet seen this side of Sylvia; this closed, shut-off person was new. She wondered how much she really knew of her. This now made two instances that Sylvia had shown another side of herself. She decided to try again and get her biggest question off her chest phrasing it in a statement that Sylvia didn't have to answer. "I haven't seen Micha amongst the helpers."

"He's not with the helpers. He stayed due to the electrical portion of the mine. He's under there with all the rest. Some thirty-odd men are buried beneath us right now. Work on your task. We need to get this done."

Gladys couldn't move. She couldn't talk. She had no breath. Mr. Davis, Mr. Kemp, and now Micha. It was all too much. She was hyperventilating when Sylvia smacked her across the face.

"They are down there, and the men up here are

doing everything they can. We need to get done so they can keep working. Pull yourself together."

Gladys nodded as she tried to compose herself.

The sting on her cheek helped ground her and the shock brought needed oxygen to her lungs. Centering herself with prayer, she joined Sylvia in silence as she focused on getting the food out as fast as she could.

CHAPTER 45

The miners took turns, working around the clock. When the women brought the food, they were thankful, but in a somber state. All the men were head-to-toe black from the coal, their expressions all the same hard-lined mouths and sunken, hollow eyes.

Gladys had learned that four miners had been brought up alive, names she didn't recognize. Three of them were badly injured and burned. A makeshift hospital had been set up in the hotel, knowing many beds may be needed.

Hours had passed and night was beginning to set in. Gladys had heard people talking about pockets of air. She didn't understand it all, but she hoped there were pockets where they could survive.

Someone had brought canaries. She had watched one get sent in ahead of a group of men and asked whoever could hear her what that was for. She didn't want the answer once she got it. Blackdamp could kill and a bird would fall first.

It was all too overwhelming. Women and children were weeping in fear. Some had left hopeless. Some stayed refusing to give up. The miners were unrelenting in their search. They wore large metal helmets that covered their whole head. Tubing came out of it to a bag that lay on their chest. Gladys learned they were oxygen helmets and were part of the equipment stored in the school.

People were speculating what had caused the explosion. So many explanations could be found. Everything from a shot placed in the wrong location to someone trying to smoke. It wasn't allowed, but Gladys overheard a few saying it was common enough they would anyway.

She hoped it didn't have anything to do with the electrical outage, but knew so little about mining she had no idea if that was even a plausible possibility.

She looked ahead to the entrance and noticed something dark black. As she watched she could make out it was an animal. The dimming light made it even harder to tell, but she thought the shape looked to be a dog. Miners were pushing it out of the way as they were moving in and out, but that creature would go right back to its post as before.

It wasn't until she ventured close that she realized it was Lady.

"Come here, girl."

She tried to get her to come to her, but Lady wouldn't leave her post. Gladys crouched down by her and buried her face in her fur. She cried and Lady let her until a car came up carrying miners and something else. Gladys took one look and had to take deep breaths to keep the vomit down. It was a person, but it no longer resembled one. Lady sniffed the air briefly before resuming her post. Gladys took that to mean it wasn't Micha.

If Micha didn't come out of this alive what would happen to Lady? She didn't want to think of that, but she couldn't help her thoughts. No one had been brought out alive for a while. Bodies were starting to surface though. Or what was left of them.

As Gladys began to tear up again the rain started to dampen everything as if the heavens were joining them all in weeping. Rain was fitting. She bet not many would even notice for a while as they were so focused on their work or too distraught in their fear.

A black cloud hung over the whole area and wouldn't lift for days to come.

CHAPTER 46

The miner's funerals were back-to-back for several days. All told, thirty-one died. One of the men that was pulled out alive later died at the hotel. A few families chose to have their loved ones' remains sent back home which shortened the number of funerals and plots to dig here. The mine owners paid for the transport and for the families to return with them. An insurance was paid out to the closest kin of all who perished.

Gladys felt numb. She had sat in the same pew for hours at a time, present in body but not mind. She had found her footing and in the blink of an eye her legs had been knocked out from under her. She had her life though. She should feel thankful for that. Maybe she was still in too much shock to be able to process it all. That was the only explanation she had for why her mind wanted to focus on herself instead of the surviving families. She felt selfish. She felt like the old Gladys and that sickened her.

Micha was pulled up with the others. His body was almost unrecognizable. Lady knew. She cried and followed his remains as far as permitted. Mr. Davis was in a similar state. Mrs. Davis was inconsolable. The worst of all was Mr. Kemp. Perhaps because he looked fine. He had coal dust all over and those that could make sense of it all said he had taken a breath as coal was in his airways. The cement box didn't shut out death. It just kept his body mostly whole while taking the life within.

Given his state of appearance from a distance, Mrs. Kemp was screaming for joy when she saw him being brought up. Gladys supposed, due to looking whole, with clothing fully intact, she thought he must be alive. It didn't take but a minute for her to register the truth. She spiraled into a full mental breakdown. They would be part of the group that chose to be sent home. Gladys hoped she could heal around her own family for she wasn't sure it could happen remaining here.

Inspectors determined the damage in the mine was extensive. There was no hope for rebuilding. It would be too costly, and it always came down to the cost for the owner. The miners had to leave, but where would they go? Where would she go? Gladys had no answers for something that was approaching. Two weeks. That was what Mary had said so many months ago. Now she was staring straight at it.

"Miss Wimble?" A man approached her that she didn't know.

"Yes?"

He cleared his throat and held something out for her. She took it but was confused when she saw it.

"Micha was going to give this to you this Christmas. It's not done yet, but I think he would have wanted you to have it anyway."

It was a ring. A thick ring, but a ring. "I don't understand."

"I'm sorry, Miss. Name's Jakub. I was a friend of Micha's. He was planning to propose this Christmas. This here is the ring he was going to use. He said he'd finish it once he knew your size."

Gladys knew Micha was serious but didn't know he was that serious. Should she accept it? Before his death she knew she wasn't going to marry him. She knew in her heart there was nothing there beyond friendship.

"Maybe this should be sent to his family. I don't even know how to contact them."

Jakub dropped his head. "It's all right. I know, and I'll be the one to make contact. Micha was one of the best men I knew. Hard worker, too. He didn't want you or anyone else to know that he couldn't read. He'd bring me his letters and I'd read them to him and write down what he wanted to say in return." He paused letting all that sink in. "They'd want you to have it. All they wanted was for him to meet a nice lady and settle down. They would have loved you. I just know it."

Gladys was touched and knew she couldn't refuse that. "What's going to happen to Lady?"

"That I don't know. She growls at all of us men."

"We'll take her!" Sadie ran up and joined in the conversation. "Oh! Can we, can we Momma?" She pleaded.

Children could bounce back so quickly. Gladys felt a tinge of jealousy towards Sadie.

"I don't suppose why not. After all she did save my Sadie's life." Mr. Crowley scooped up his daughter and settled her on his shoulders. She patted his head, messing his hair in excitement, which made them all chuckle. It was the first of any laughter since the explosion and it felt right.

Jakub nodded a bit and thought it over. "I think that's fitting. I know Sadie had a special place in Micha's heart. She'd be his pick of who'd take her if he was here to do so."

That brought everyone's mood back to the present. Mr. Crowley and Jakub shook hands and Jakub left the little family to go speak with other miners.

Gladys waited until they made it back to the Crowley's home to ask Sylvia what she thought she should do. Gladys had a big decision to make. Finding a post in the middle of the school year was bound to be difficult, but the alternative would be moving back home. She didn't know what to do, or how to go about making that big of a decision. She waited until everyone settled in, including Lady, who curled up in front of the fire Mr. Crowley made. It seemed Lady felt just as much at home here as she did with Micha.

"Why doesn't she come with us, Momma?" Sadie again seemed to have all the answers at the tip of her tongue.

Jeffrey could be heard mumbling under his breath about how awful it would be having a teacher traveling with them. He was certain she'd take all the fun out of it.

"Kids, shush." She glared at Jeffrey before turning back to Sadie, "This isn't just taking in a dog. This is Gladys. She needs to figure out her path on her own."

Gladys was concerned. She knew everyone had to leave, but she just realized that meant she would be separated from the only real family she had ever known. "Where are you going?"

"You don't know, dear? I do remember telling you while on our trip to Tacoma where we would go next should we need to leave here."

Gladys thought back for a minute. "Indiana! That's a long way away."

Sylvia nodded. Sadie chimed in, "We get to ride the train!"

Gladys smiled down at her. "I bet that will be exciting."

Sylvia watched the two of them talk about the train ride. "You could, you know."

Gladys snapped her head back. "I could what?"

"Come with us."

She thought a bit before firmly shaking her head no. "I shouldn't. My parents will want me home. Besides, where would I work?" It all seemed so outrageous to her. She couldn't just hop on a train and take off across the country, could she? Isn't that exactly what she did to get here?"

"You already did it once. What's the difference?"

"I had a job to go to."

Sylvia smiled and softened a bit. "And now you have a family to go with. A job will come. Don't worry about that. Come with us. Worst-case scenario: you hate it and go back to Montana. Besides, I really feel this was all part of the plan. All His will. Why else would we have met? Just to be ripped apart? I don't believe that. I think He placed you here for a reason."

His will? Why would He have allowed me to come if not to meet them and find everything I've ever wanted just to end up where I started? He knew what would happen. Yet He put me here anyway.

Gladys was just beginning to understand His true ways, but she knew enough to know He wouldn't have caused the explosion, killing all those men. He would have mourned the loss right alongside all of His people.

Could something good really come from moving here? From being here at this time?

Gladys was giddy inside, realizing she really could do that. She was being kicked out of town here and she didn't want to go back to Deer Lodge. She loved these people and they loved her. She felt a mixture of nervousness and excitement swirled together. "Do you know much about the town?"

The Crowley's all laughed. Mr. Crowley answered. "I know my brother and his family. That's enough for me. And you know us, which should be enough for you."

"What will you be doing? Do you have work?" He wiped his face, "That I do. My brother owns a feed store. He'll put me to work and there's living quarters upstairs. It'll be tight, as they live up there, too, but I'm sure it can't be as tight as we have it here now."

Gladys mulled all that over. She didn't like the thoughts that came first to her mind. Sleeping with Sadie might be a reality. She not only knew she could do it, she knew she would.

Gladys had realized that friendships and true family were treasures to hold close. They could be lost forever in the blink of an eye and she would do what she could to make sure she held onto what she had left for as long as God allowed.

It would be a new leaf. She had found a family and she would follow them anywhere. She held the wooden ring tightly in her palm and thanked God for the time she had with Micha. He helped her learn what friendship was and she would never forget that, or him, or how quickly things could change. Jumping head first sometimes was necessary. Taking your time could make you lose it all.

"All right. I'll go."

The house erupted in cheers and a group hug turned into a dog pile as Lady tried to join in and tripped Sadie, setting off a chain reaction. They all laid on the floor laughing and thanking God that Laly was tucked into her bassinet and not on the floor with them.

Gladys couldn't believe she was doing it, but at the same time she didn't know why she ever hesitated. She started this adventure hoping to find her own way, carve a new name into her future, bloom into the prettiest flower she could, and leave the past, and all who dragged her down behind her.

She had thought circumstances had proven failure, but now she knew she succeeded more than she ever thought possible. She found a true home, not the one with walls and doors, but the one with hands and hearts. Hands for helping guide and shape her into her best self and hearts to love her as the imperfect person she was. She found home.

When their best laid-plans crumble, two women set out of personal journeys to find their true paths.

CLICK HERE to begin A Proper Love, the next installment of Hardships of the Heart!

WHAT'S NEXT?

**Read the first chapter of A PROPER LOVE, book 4
of the Hardships of the Heart series...**

Gladys Wimble had just finished cataloging the
latest seed arrival when Jeffrey and Sadie bounded
through the office doors with the long-haired mutt,
Lady dog, hot on their trail. Jeffrey had clearly been
running, as evidenced by his tousled chestnut hair
and beads of sweet on his forehead. Sadie's raven
pigtails kept moving long after she had stopped. The
children excitedly shouted in unison that she had a
letter. Gladys took the envelope from Sadie's hands
and thanked them both before excusing all three
back upstairs to their living quarters.

Several people lived above the Crowley Feed and Seed, all of whom were blood-related except for Gladys. In all her childhood she never dreamt she'd end up working at a feed and seed, living hundreds of miles from home, and calling people family she'd known less than two years.

"Are the children all right?" Sylvia poked her head into the office.

"Yes, they are fine. They delivered a letter from my mother." She held up said letter and sighed.

Sylvia gave a knowing, comforting smile and left Gladys alone. Letters from Gladys' mother were never pleasant. Some were better than others, but they always had the same theme; find a husband and return to her roots. Mrs. Wimble loathed Gladys' decision to become a working woman. Gladys loved it. She loved it so much, in fact, that now she was doing it for free. Working at the Feed and Seed in lieu of paying for room and board, plus a little pocket change, helped her self-proclaimed adopted family. Volunteering her time at a few local elementary schools here in New Albany, Indiana fed her heart.

Gladys used the letter opener that rested in a cup on the desk. She mentally tried to prepare herself for the onslaught that was on the pages. Living here awhile now, so far from where she grew up in Deer Lodge, Montana, meant she had several letters, each a bit more desperate than the last. She could have never prepared herself for what this one said.

Dearest Gladys,

I hope this letter finds you well. Of course, in just a short time I should know that answer for myself. You have talked up this new city you live in so much in your previous letters that you've piqued my interest. Your father and I have decided that I should come see you and stay for a while. I would like to see firsthand where my daughter is living and what she is doing and spend a bit of time together. It has been too long. Now, I don't know how long I will be there, nor do I know precisely when I shall arrive, but know it will be soon. I would like to stay with you. I hope that is fine and that you have the room to house your mother. You did say you were living in a quaint apartment that overlooked the Ohio River. It does sound lovely. I will send a note informing you of my arrival time when I know.

Your excited mother

"No, no, no!" Gladys flipped the paper over hoping to see more, something about the letter being a joke, or that maybe her father changed his mind and realized the horribleness of the idea. Nothing was there. She stood and paced as far as the office would let her, which wasn't far, given the large desk, filing cabinets, and chairs that took up the space. She was feeling a mixture of emotions that could only be summed up by comparing them to a cyclone. Anger, frustration, worry, dread, fear: they were all swirling around in her head and chest. She pushed through the door and made her way into the main floor of the store, dodging barrels and crates as she headed for the door.

"Gladys, are you heading out?" Nancy was a sweet and short lady. She married Mr. Crowley, the store owner. Not to be confused with Mr. Crowley, the brother married to Sylvia. Both men told her to call them by their Christian names, but she was still having a hard time completely breaking from her upbringing. She had changed so much, but certain stubborn things clung to her.

Gladys pushed down her emotions before turning and responding. "Yes, ma'am. If that's all right. I did finish the cataloging of the seed order. I thought a breath of fresh air would be lovely."

"I could go for a quick walk." Sylvia was returning from being upstairs with the children.

Gladys took a breath and pushed her feelings down a bit farther, as she really wanted to be alone. Both women walked out into the sun and paused, letting the rays hug their skin. Gladys set the pace and chose to walk towards the river. Sylvia followed, but remained quiet. Gladys knew she wanted to discuss the letter. They always talked after a letter came. Sylvia had a way with reminding Gladys that this was her life, not her mother's. She helped her stay firm.

New Albany was full of life in the middle of the day. Automobiles were everywhere which were amazing to see. Boat traffic was heavy on the river and people were running to and fro, loading and unloading shipments from them. Trains were frequent and they crossed over the bridge into Kentucky carrying freight and passengers. Large factories with smoke towers dotted the shoreline. There weren't many shops in this area. Those were downtown, a few streets to the north. Given the option, she preferred to be by the river than in the middle of the shops.

New Albany had wealth unlike any Gladys had known. Back home she was in the upper class. Here, her parents would have been more middle class. Gladys liked the less rigid, more relaxed way of the people who frequented the river as opposed to the uppity downtowners. The sense of community was palpable in this area.

There was more life at night than in the two other towns in which she'd lived. Deer Lodge was the closest in comparison but was much smaller. They didn't have the specialty shops or activities that could be found here.

She couldn't find anything to compare with Ravensdale, Washington. That town was small, brown, and trying, and would stay in her heart for as long as she lived. Gladys had found herself in that sleepy little mining community. She'd found the Crowleys there. Ravensdale would always be her favorite place to live even though it had been her hardest.

"I know you are waiting for me to tell you what mother wanted this time. I'm afraid to say this letter is nothing like her others."

Sylvia's eyes widened in surprise. In the almost two years she'd been working with Sylvia, every letter was the same. "Did she finally decide to give up and let you live the way you want to?"

Gladys laughed, full-on belly laughed. "Oh, that's funny. I've rarely known my mother to quit anything. No. She is coming."

"Coming! Here?" Sylvia stopped dead in her tracks, her brown eyes shot wide open, and an auburn curl subtly bobbed when she snapped her head.

"Yes, I'm afraid so. She wants to stay with me also."

"But where? We are so full already."

This was true. Mr. David Crowley and his wife Nancy owned the Feed and Seed. They had one short-for-his-age son, Sam, aged ten, and blonde twin girls, Flossie and Sophie, or Flo and So, aged seven. Mr. James Crowley and his wife Sylvia had Jeffrey, who was eight, Sadie, who was six, and baby Laly. Along with Gladys, that made for a full house and tight quarters.

Most of the children slept in bunk beds in one room with the boys on one side and the girls on the other. A divider sheet had been hung from the ceiling dividing the space equally. The exception was Laly, James and Sylvia's youngest, who slept with them. Gladys had her own room that was tiny, but much better than her first year in Ravensdale when she had to bunk with other families. David and Nancy had the room at the end of the hall and James and Sylvia had partitioned off a portion of the living space to be their room. Eventually everyone hoped that James and Sylvia would find a home of their own, but for now the situation had to work. Traveling ate up finances and James hadn't yet to save enough for that next step.

"I suppose we could do like the children's room and put a bunk bed in mine. Mother could have the top." Both ladies almost fell over laughing. Gladys' mother would have never stayed in such conditions. Thinking about the reaction that would undoubtedly cause issues made Gladys want to seriously consider that option.

Sylvia pounded on her chest, working to catch her breath. "There is a bigger problem, I'm thinking, than where your mother will sleep. David is a wonderful man. James and David are so much alike. He will expect some work from her, though."

Gladys turned and stared out across the river. "When will she be here?"

"I'm not sure. All she said was soon."

"Well, that must mean she hasn't purchased her passage yet which gives us some time to prepare. Maybe you could write to her and explain the housing situation. Maybe she will have another idea."

Gladys moaned. "I could, but I sort of already

told her that I live in a lovely quaint apartment over-looking the river. I didn't mention it was above a business and that I live with people."

"Oh, dear. That does make this a bit more difficult."

"I could move." Gladys was grasping at straws now. She knew she couldn't move. She didn't have the finances for that.

"And just where would you go and how would you pay for that?" Sylvia chewed her lip, "Are there no schools here hiring? This city sure has a number of them."

"No, I'm afraid not. Maybe by this summer something will open up, but for now I'm continuing to volunteer and waiting for any opportunity."

"Well, we are getting nowhere going in circles out here just the two of us. Why don't we go back and talk with James? Maybe he'll have an idea we haven't yet thought of."

Sylvia wrapped one arm around Gladys and the two walked back to the Feed and Seed. Sylvia was determined that a solution could be found. Gladys had all but given up hope.

What happens next? Don't wait to find out...

A Proper Love is now available.

CLICK HERE to get your copy so that you can keep reading this series today!

MEET THE AUTHOR

Stefanie Bridges-Mikota grew up in a small town in southwestern Washington where she learned timeless values. She married her high school sweetheart and they are now raising their children in the kind of happily-ever-after that often happens in books.

Although middle age is creeping up far too quickly, Stefanie is still trying to decide what to do when she grows up. She has worked in a variety of fields, each one another stepping stone on the path to being a published author.

MORE FROM STEFANIE BRIDGES-MIKOTA

Hardships of the Heart

A Proper Heart

A Proper Home

A Proper Family

A Proper Love

Fragile Flowers

Mending Broken Hearts

Penning Perfect Love

Shifting Future Dreams

The Pioneer Brides of Rattlesnake Ridge

Approaching from Arizona

Letters from Home

Letters from Washington

Printed in Great Britain
by Amazon